IN CLEAR
SIGHT

JUDITH TIPPING

Copyright © 2023 Judith Tipping

All rights reserved.

No part of this book may be reproduced, or stored in a retrieval system, or transmitted in any form or by any means, electronic, mechanical, photocopying, recording, or otherwise, without express written permission of the publisher.

ISBN: 9798850740498
Second Edition

First edition published 2022

Cover: Canva
Formatting: Elaine Denning

For my dad, Les Lumby, who is always in
my heart.

And for Julie Mayers Alejo, who read my manuscript
a hundred times or more. X

PROLOGUE
1981

Tracy squealed with delight as she poked and poked again at the shiny plastic face, using the blunt ended paper scissors from her card making set, until she finally managed to push the eyes out of her sister's favourite doll. She smiled as the long pieces of golden hair fell to the floor as she cut it off in random chunks, leaving the head with nothing but a few rat's tails. Then she tipped the contents of her pencil case on to her sister's bed and picked out a thick black felt tip pen. She laughed as she drew a pair of glasses on to the face where the doll's beautiful crystal blue eyes had been, and she continued to laugh as she added a black moustache above the top lip of the doll's perfect mouth. She replaced the lid on the pen and put everything back into the pencil case and then once again she picked up the scissors and carefully cut the doll's pretty silver dress into rags, watching with interest as the pieces of material landed on the top of the dolls hair that was already lying on the floor.

Tracy sat there for a few minutes and admired her work and then she abandoned the doll, leaving it lying haphazardly on her sister's pillow. She went back to her own bedroom and sat down on the floor. As she leaned backwards on her bed with both knees tucked up in front of her, she thought about what she had done to her sister's beloved doll and how it served her right.

She's always leaving me on my own, while she goes to her friend's house for sleepovers, or 'pyjama parties', as she likes to call them.

Tracy reached for a pad and a pencil and shuffled around to grab a book to lean on. She needed to plan her evening at home with her stupid boring parents.

That would be another surprise for her sister when she gets home tomorrow

CHAPTER ONE
2003

Anne Holland squirted honey on to each pancake before rolling them into a tube and putting one on each plate. She filled two glasses with orange juice and looked at her watch - time was precious in the morning. She leaned on the banister and called up the stairs, "Girls, your breakfasts are ready on the table, I'm just going for my run. And, yes, before you ask, I will be back in time to take you to school."

She smiled to herself as she heard the two girls bickering over how much time the other one had spent in the bathroom. She didn't expect or wait for any replies as she closed the front door behind her and set off in the direction of Lakeland Wood.

As she began to pick up the pace, she breathed in the coolness of the frosty air and even though it was still quite dark, the frost that lay sparkling like a dusting of icing sugar, created a brightness which enabled her to see clearly. Thankfully though, it wasn't slippery under foot.

She veered off to the left and followed a pathway that would take her through the park, then she would be faced with the challenge of Seaton Hill, known locally as Cardiac Hill, which would lead her into the woods. She ran this same route every morning, whatever the weather delivered. She loved the exercise, it left her feeling uplifted, both mentally and physically.

As she reached the top of the hill and entered the woodland she stopped and looked behind her, pausing for a moment to take in the magical view. She basked in the magnificent sight in front of her and she watched as the dawn began to break, and the rising sun started to beam its warm smile across the horizon. Anne let out a contented sigh and thought to herself how good life was.

Continuing on her way, she began to concentrate on her breathing. She heard a branch crack and glanced over to her right and behind her but there was no one in sight. As she continued jogging at a steady pace, following the twists and the curves of the pathway, she couldn't shake the feeling of unease that was scrambling around in the pit of her stomach. She stopped again and looked behind her.

There was no one there. Her mind was playing tricks on her.

She shook her head and laughed to herself as she turned back and came face to face with a hooded person.

A gloved hand was across her mouth before she could scream. She tried to bring her leg up and kick out at whoever this was, but they were quick and before she had a chance to react, she felt something tight around her throat. Her mind was struggling to deal with what was happening as her fingers grappled at her neck in an attempt to rid it of whatever it was that was trying to squeeze the life out of her. She tried to speak; she wanted to plead for her life. Surely if she spoke, if her pleas could be heard, it would stop this person. But no words came out of her mouth.

She began to feel disorientated, and panic filled her entire body as her eyes felt like they were going to burst out of their sockets. She kicked and she punched but try as she might she was no match for her attacker, and as muted hysteria continued to bolt through her, Anne's thoughts began to ricochet between her two beautiful daughters and her wonderful husband.

She struggled to breathe, and she struggled to swallow as saliva leaked out and dripped down from the sides of her mouth. Anne had always been a fighter and she had fought hard all of her life to get the things she wanted, but right now, in this moment, she knew this was it, that her life was about to be extinguished and although she had fought back with every ounce of strength that she could muster she knew it was not going to be enough.

Tears spilled over her bulging eyes and even though the sun was beginning to show its face, for Anne it was not light but only darkness that engulfed her.

Her body suddenly felt very heavy. A heaviness that only death could bring, as the life drained out of it, and she exhaled her last breath.

CHAPTER TWO

I watched intensely as her eyes that had held all the panic finally surrendered, and, as she accepted her inevitable fate, they relaxed into a fixed stare.

The show was over.

The grand finale.

The curtain had closed!

I laughed out loud at my theatrical outburst, as feelings of elation conflicted with waves of sadness. A mixed-up mash of emotions flushed through my body and left me feeling euphoric. The best bit was over - that final moment of submission when her eyes had begged me to reconsider and allow her to continue her crusade with life and achieve all of her hopes and dreams.

It was breath-taking – literally, and again I laughed.

My own breathing however was so loud it filled my head as short sharp breaths began pumping boundlessly in the space between my throat and my chest. My heart was banging so ferociously I couldn't hear anything else. The adrenaline was spinning through my veins like a tornado, and it left me feeling dizzy.

The others before her would remain a secret forever untold - but this one would be different because for the first time this one would be found and not because that arrogant shit, DCI Strain, is clever enough to find her, but simply because I wanted her body to be discovered. It was finally time to let him see my work - like a show case of an upcoming movie. I had wanted to up my game and increase the thrill, to make it riskier, and I had achieved my goal and risen to the challenge admirably.

I was closer to home and on a route that I used, myself, to jog. I really hoped somebody would find her before I did - how embarrassing would that be.

I laughed as I released the ends of the chiffon scarf and she slumped backwards onto the ground. Her fight was over, she was gone. I breathed in the silence as I folded the scarf into a neat triangle and placed it over her eyes.

I straightened up and rubbed my shoulder - she had been a feisty one.

I kicked some loose bracken and leaves over her, and then I walked away leaving the lifeless corpse scarcely covered over in her temporary grave and made my way out of the woodland, stopping only to remove my gloves. I shoved them into a black bag and screwed up the top.

The walk back to my car was uneventful; there wasn't anyone around. I rummaged in my pocket for the key fob and when I pressed it the car lit up. The boot opened automatically, and I placed the bag inside another and lined it up neatly next to my tool kit.

I closed the boot and took a last look around. What a beautiful morning.

I checked my watch. I felt pleased that I still had enough time to get home and have a shower before work. I started the engine and pushed my favourite Queen CD into the player and boomed up the volume.

CHAPTER THREE

As the alarm clock sprang noisily into life Sherry Taylor stretched and turned over in bed. Her fingers hunted out the *snooze* button and pressed down hard as subconsciously her mind began working – it was Tuesday, and her first call wasn't until 9 a.m. She struggled to half open one eye and could see that it was 6.45. *No rush then.* She turned over and drifted back off to sleep.

It seemed like only a few seconds later when Sherry stirred again as the shrill sound of the alarm clock invaded her head for the second time that morning, and once again, she began to mentally sift through the fine details of the day that lay ahead, this time though, she opened her eyes and stretched from head to toe as she looked around her bedroom. Bright sunshine was peeping through the slight gap in the centre of the curtains where she hadn't quite pulled them together and it had created a bright line that lit up and spliced her bedroom in two. She threw back the quilt and slid out of bed and as she stretched her arms high above her head, she walked over to the window and pulled open the curtains.

It was a beautiful October morning, and she could see a light frost was glistening on the ground. Sherry loved autumn; it was always full of beautiful colours. She loved how the leaves turned from healthy green to crinkly brown and dropped from their boughs, littering the pathways, reminding her of her childhood walking to school with her friends and how they had kicked the leaves around together. She smiled at the distant memory as she stood there in her warm bedroom.

Sherry headed for the bathroom and had a hot shower. As she brushed her hair and pulled it into a tight pony tail, she grumbled to herself, 'I wish my nails grew as fast as my hair did,' and she made a mental note to make an appointment with her hairdresser. She applied a minimum amount of make-up and after shuffling through the hangers in her wardrobe she chose a pair of grey trousers and a dusky pink cashmere sweater. Happy with her choices she dressed and went downstairs.

In the kitchen she opened a cupboard and eyed the various cereal boxes. She finally settled on porridge. Thomas furred up against her legs in a bid to remind her that he too was awake and also needed his breakfast.

"Hello, my beautiful boy," she said as she picked up her cat and snuggled him to her. He purred loudly as he rubbed his face under her chin. "Are you hungry too?" Sherry obliged him with his favourite food and made herself a bowl of instant porridge, topping it off with a drizzle of honey. She switched on the television and sat on the sofa. She liked to watch the morning news and the weather forecast.

The breaking news this morning was the discovery of a body in Lakeland Woods. A white female believed to be in her early thirties had been found by an unsuspecting jogger at 7.15 this morning. Sherry found herself wondering which would be worse; to be dead or to find a dead body. She concluded that obviously both would be quite harrowing.

"Not a great start to the day for either of them, eh, Thomas" she said, as she stood up and dumped her breakfast bowl, unwashed, in the sink.

She put on her coat and a pair of black ankle boots and glanced over at the cat, who by this time, was already curled up asleep - she picked up her bag and closed the front door behind her.

The traffic had not been too bad, so Sherry had arrived at her first appointment in good time. She turned the key in the front door and opened it. As she did so she called out, "Morning Mrs Johnson, it's only me, Sherry, I'm coming in; call off the guard dogs."

This always made Mrs Johnson laugh because Sherry said the same thing every day.

"I'm in the bedroom, love," she called back; "come on through." Likewise, her answer made Sherry laugh, because Mrs Johnson was bedridden so she always knew where she would be.

She took off her coat and boots and slipped on a pair of flat, comfortable shoes that she always left inside the front door before she made her way along the hallway and pushed open the door into the bedroom. She gave Mrs Johnson a big hug. Sherry loved this woman like she was her own Mother.

"You look lovely as usual this morning." Sherry smiled at her. "How are you?"

"I'm as well as I can hope to be at my age, love," Mrs Johnson said, as she hugged her back.

"What would you like for your breakfast today?"

"I fancy an omelette if that's okay?"

"Of course. You can have whatever you want, you know that!" Sherry replied.

"I don't know what I would do without you:" The old lady looked lovingly at her. "You are my ray of sunshine in what would otherwise be a drab day."

"And I don't know what I would do without you either," Sherry said sincerely. "First things first though, shall we get the nitty-gritty done before breakfast; bed bath, change your nightdress etc."

"You're the boss, love, so whatever you say."

A little over an hour later Sherry presented Mrs Johnson with a tray that had an omelette, two slices of toast with butter and a cup of tea on it. She left her to eat her breakfast and went back to the kitchen. The washing machine was in its final spin, so she tidied up and carried the ironing board into the bedroom. Mrs Johnson liked to chat with Sherry whilst she did the ironing. She was on her own most of the day, so it was nice for her to have some company. As Sherry skilfully glided the iron around the fluted buttons on a thick cotton nightdress, Mrs Johnson said, "Did you see the news earlier about that poor young woman, who was found dead in the woods? Apparently, she was out jogging. They are saying she had a husband and two young daughters. It's so tragic."

"Yes, I did, it's awful isn't it? You go out for a jog, and you don't ever come home." Sherry frowned. "It's a bit too local for my liking. Lakeland Woods are only about twenty miles away."

"It's so sad, such a terrible waste of a young life." Mrs Johnson's eyes welled up as she looked tenderly at Sherry and said, "I don't want you to go jogging, Sherry; I don't want anything bad to happen to you."

"Honestly, you don't have anything to worry about - there is no fear of me going jogging, I'm far too lazy."

Mrs Johnson scoffed and said, "I don't think you and the word lazy would ever fit into the same sentence together - how could you think that? You don't stop for a minute when you are here."

Sherry collected the breakfast dishes and washed them up. She put the ironing board away and came back in with a tray laid out with freshly made sandwiches and a couple of fairy cakes, all wrapped individually in cling film, and placed it down on the bedside table for Mrs Johnson's lunch. Then she refilled the teas-made and restocked the biscuit tin. "There you are. Plenty of nibbles to keep you going for a few hours. Is there anything else you need?" she asked as she gave Mrs Johnson another hug.

Mrs Johnson shook her head.

"In that case then I will see you later for tea at the usual time - around four-thirty."

"Okay love. Bye for now."

Sherry sat in her car and took five minutes to fill in her notes before she drove off to her next call.

CHAPTER FOUR

The autumn weeks drifted on by and the cold sunny days that came hand in hand with October had now been replaced with the long, drab days of November. They were filled with a constant mist of drizzle. Although slightly milder, this type of day remained trapped in a gloomy dusk which never got to enjoy the full light of day. I called them moody days, because they form the day ahead and influence people's minds, leaving them without motivation to do anything or go anywhere.

I was parked in a lay-by on the edge of a nearby town. The view from here was excellent because it overlooked the park on the other side of the road. This particular park was stunning, with its beautiful lake and wooden benches where people were sitting together and chatting with their loved ones.

There was an area of woodland to the right of the lake and grassland to the left, and sitting here, I could witness the arrival of a murkier light as it bounded towards early evening darkness bringing the remnants of the daytime to a close. People were beginning to head off to the warmth and comfort of their homes and all that were left behind were dog walkers and bike riders. These people were no good to me as they tended to walk or ride in small groups. No. My interest lay with the joggers because these people, more often than not, chose to run on their own. Of course, I usually had a specific target, but they were also excellent for a random kill, if ever the mood took me, and in the past, I had used them to practice on before I started on my list. Generally, they were an easy target, with their music plugged into their ears rendering them deaf to any surrounding noise. In a way, I could relate to them wanting to shut the world out, to be able to escape from disappointment and be totally engulfed in their own passion for freedom and solitude and run wherever they wanted to and listen to the music they loved without being controlled. I hated that word; 'control' and I began to shake as resentment hitched a lift with the blood in my veins so it could travel faster and be catapulted to where it needed to be. Although I tried hard to keep these dreadful thoughts from my mind, it was difficult. As they began to march in like an army of soldiers invading my mind there was no stopping them and my head became so full that there wasn't any room left for rational thinking. Vengeance was the only emotion I could feel as I got out of the car and slammed the door shut. Driven by fury, I opened the boot, grabbed a black bag, and jogged off across the road in the direction of the park.

My spine shivered with excitement as I breathed in the night air. I had never been afraid of the dark and I watched from the shadows as the park emptied, and then jogged off into the woodland. I saw the figure of a girl jogging towards me and smirked.

Excellent! There she is, right on time.

I stretched out my fingers which felt restricted by the tight new leather gloves. I knelt down and fiddled around with my trainer, and I looked around. There wasn't a soul in sight except for her. My heart was pumping faster and faster as I ventured slightly off the path. I took a chiffon scarf from out of the black bag and shoved it into my pocket.

I remained in sight as I waited, hardly able to contain my rising excitement.

As my intended victim passed me by, I called out, "Excuse me!" but she didn't answer. "Excuse me!" I said again, only louder this time, but she didn't even turn around.

God damn it! What was wrong with people? What made them think that it was okay to be so rude? It wasn't like she couldn't see me.

With my lips pursed tightly together I raced after her and as I came up behind her, I lunged and crashed the piece of wood that I had picked up down onto her skull. As she fell to the ground, I rolled her over to face me. "It's rude to be so ignorant!" I shouted in her face. "You should speak when you're spoken to! Couldn't you see that I was waiting for you? Wasn't it obvious?"

The look on her face was one of total shock. She had no idea what had just happened to her. She struggled desperately and her legs flailed around in a frenzied attempt to escape my attack. To my surprise, she managed to break free from my tight grip and she rolled over onto her hands and feet, but as she tried to get up, I grabbed her ankle and twisted it sharply. She let out a shrill scream. Consumed with anger I strengthened my grip on her and smashed the piece of wood down onto the back of her knee. Once again, she cried out. In a flash I was on her, and I turned her back over so that she was facing me. As the physical strength drained from her, she stopped screaming and looked me straight in the eyes. "Please" she begged. "Please don't hurt me."

She looked pathetic with a flow of tears leaking down onto her cheeks. "Really?" I said, and I wanted to laugh, "Is that all you've got?"

Feeling no compassion for this girl, I kept smashing the piece of wood down onto her skull until finally she lay there still and silent.

Breathing hard I dragged her into the undergrowth. Both of the plugs had fallen out of her ears, but they were still attached to her device, and I could hear 'Rock-a-bye Baby' by Clean Bandit playing as the song filtered into the evening air. I stood up straight and shook my head in despair as I realised what a mess I had made, why hadn't I been more patient? Usually, I strangled my target slowly and precisely so I could savour the moment their life drained away and soak up the agonising pain in their eyes, but I had killed her too quickly and only heard her pleading, which wasn't enough to satisfy me.

God, I'm so stupid.

I pulled angrily at the chiffon scarf that was stashed in my pocket and neatly folded it into a triangle. After placing it over her eyes, I kicked a few clumps of fallen leaves over her dead body in a half-hearted attempt to hide her.

My breathing was erratic as I ran back to where I had dropped the black bag, I took off my coat and gloves and pushed them inside it, then, with a last look around I picked it up and jogged back to my car. My hands were clenching alternatively into fists as I got into the driver's seat. I sat there for a few minutes breathing deeply in an attempt to compose myself, then I started the engine and drove off.

Typically, this route home only took about thirty minutes, but the traffic was heavier than normal this evening, which left me slightly puzzled. Rush- hour was generally done with by now, so why the increased traffic. Perhaps there were road works ahead. Then I remembered that the premier of *Lord of the Rings: Return of the King* was showing at Cine-world tonight. Maybe I should go. I had enjoyed the books.

When I finally arrived home, I had a hot shower, but I couldn't settle. I had an unfulfilled feeling deep down inside, so I did my hair and make-up and sifted through my wardrobe. I chose a provocative black dress and stood in front of the mirror as I admired myself.

With a smile of approval, I put on my coat, picked up my bag and keys and locked my front door behind me.

CHAPTER FIVE

Detective Chief Inspector Strain was standing with his hands in his pockets, fiddling with some loose change that lay in the bottom of one of them. As he studied the incident board, he stared at the pictures of the two dead women pinned up in front of him. The first victim was a thirty-two-year-old woman named Anne Holland. She had been strangled whilst out on an early morning run. She left behind a husband, two young daughters and two broken-hearted elderly parents. The second victim: Jenna Hopkins, was twenty-two years old. She had also left behind a grieving family, of both parents and a younger brother. She had fallen victim whilst out on an evening run, when she was violently beaten to death by a number of blows to her head with a piece of wood. This was discovered at the crime scene after it had been discarded, presumably by the murderer, who clearly knew what he was doing because apart from the murder weapon, there were no other traces of evidence found at the scene. Both of the young women had been murdered within six weeks of each other.

"I hope this isn't the start of a serial killer!" he said out loud, as he turned to face Rob, his DS.

Rob was twenty-eight years old and a bright young lad, but a bit green when it came to homicide. He had only recently been transferred, at his own request, from the fraud squad which was a totally different type of policing.

DCI Strain threw his hands into the air and let out a sigh. He was passionate about his job, but he was easily frustrated when things didn't go his way. "Well, I don't know, two girls in as many months; they didn't know each other, they didn't look like each other and they didn't share the same boyfriend! There's no apparent motive. The only thing they had in common, as far as we know, is the fact that they were both murdered while they were out jogging. Not much to go on, is it Rob?"

"No Guv," Rob replied, not offering anything more to the table.

Strain thought for a moment and then said, "Come on, let's call it a night. I'll see you tomorrow. Unless you fancy a drink?"

"Sorry Guv," Rob said as he powered down his computer, "I've already got plans for tonight, maybe later in the week though." He slipped his jacket on and added, "See you tomorrow."

It was times like this that Strain missed his former assistant, Andy. They had been colleagues for ten years and had become good friends in their personal life too until Andy had met and fallen in love with an Australian lady called Beverley. He had moved to the other side of the world to be with her, leaving Strain a 'Billie no-mates.' Strain came to realise, as he got older, that it was more difficult to meet people who would become good friends, male or female. He took one last look at the incident board with its huge lack of information on it and sighed. He ran his fingers through his hair, switched off the lights and closed the office door behind him.

"Goodnight Trevor," he called out as he walked past reception.

"Goodnight Guv," the duty officer replied as Strain left the building.

Outside Strain crossed the road and headed towards his local, 'The Golden Goose Inn', which was about a ten-minute walk away. He had been using it for years and although it wasn't the most exciting Pub, he knew he would find company in there. As he pushed open the door and went inside, his face met with a welcome rush of warm air. He looked around and swiftly did a recce of the room. He was well known in the bar and the tender handed him his usual, Scotch and water. Strain pulled out a stool, sat on it and finished his drink. He gestured to the barman for a refill, and then for another. As he looked around at the people who were chatting and laughing together, he envied them their ignorance. Looking at dead bodies on a regular basis took its toll on your sense of humour, but a couple of Scotches usually helped. He swished his drink around the glass before knocking the third one back. The tension in his shoulders began to disperse as the alcohol started to kick in and work its magic.

Strain pushed his bar stool back and stood up. But as he did so he suddenly became aware of a loud shriek in his ear. He spun around to find that he had pushed it onto a lady's foot: "Oh Christ, I'm sorry," he said and quickly grabbed at the offending piece of furniture. Her crumpled face and the row of swear words that tumbled out of her mouth said it all and although Strain tried hard to hold back, he was unsuccessful and he burst out laughing: "Can I get you a painkiller?" he asked, putting on his favourite boyish grin.

"Well, you sure know how to spoil a girl, don't you? Okay then. As long as it comes in the form of a Bacardi and Coke with ice." She laughed tentatively. "I'm Christie."

"Strain," he said and held out his hand in a mock introduction.

"What; no first name?"

"Sorry, it comes with the job. Surnames rule in my trade. I'm Martin." He turned back to the bar and ordered them both a drink and then he helped her onto the stool. "I really am sorry. Does it hurt much?"

"No, not now. It was just a shock to have my toe flattened. It's buzzing a bit, but I feel quite sure that you are going to make me forget all about it!"

Strain noticed that she said this with a provocatively, sexy smile on her face, and as he handed her the Bacardi, he was quick to realise that she was flirting with him. She was a good-looking woman, and he was as horny as hell, so he didn't want to blow it.

"Well, if pushing a bar stool out without looking means I get to talk to a lovely lady like you, then I'm all for it," he said smoothly.

She blushed slightly and smiled at him as she mixed the bottle of cola with her Bacardi and swished it round. "So, Surnames rule in your trade… What is it that you do when you're not breaking toes?"

Here goes.

"I'm a cop," he said nervously as he studied her face. He was never sure how people were going to react to this information, but apparently, he didn't need to worry because she came straight back with a teasing reply.

"I hope you're going to put your uniform on for me, Sergeant?"

She said it in such an arousing way that he thought he would like to take her right there and then. He leaned into her and caught the aroma of her perfume, as he said in a quiet, husky voice, "I think that can definitely be arranged."

They finished their drinks and left the bar together.

The screaming sound of the alarm clock barged uninvited, into Strain's head and gave him a rude awakening.

He reached his arm out from under the duvet and silenced the intrusive noise and then he turned his attention to the woman who was lying next to him. Her golden blonde hair lay dishevelled across her face. He gently pushed it back and kissed her lightly on her cheek and then moved his lips upwards and kissed her on her ear. She responded instantly by slipping her hand around his waist and pulling him firmly to her. There was no encouragement necessary, he couldn't think of a better way to start the day.

Strain got up first. He had a shower, wrapped a towel around his waist and headed into the kitchen to make two coffees which he took into the bedroom. He stared at the empty bed. He was disappointed to find that she had already left, but there was a note lying on his pillow that she had written in red lipstick.

See you around xx

He smiled to himself as he got dressed, drank both cups of coffee, and left his flat. It was a crisp cold morning, but the sun was warm on his face. He felt better than he had in days as he got into his car and drove to work.

CHAPTER SIX

"Hello, Mrs Alderson, it's me," Sherry spoke slowly into the speaker box on the wall and waited for a response, but impatience got the better of her. "Hello! Can you hear me?"

"Please speak slowly and clearly or I can't understand what you are saying!" Mrs Alderson's irritable voice came back through the speaker.

Sherry rolled her eyes and repeated herself, with a voice almost robot like. "Hello, Mrs Alderson, it's me Sherry!"

A loud click followed, and the front door opened automatically. Mrs Alderson was nothing like Mrs Johnson, she was sour faced with a stern mannerism. Mrs Johnson had initially began her working life as a midwife and then several years later she had changed her vocation and trained to be a nursery nurse, which might account for her overly generous and compassionate nature. Mrs Alderson, however, had been a headmistress at an all-girls school and she had an abrupt and somewhat serious attitude. In general, she was not much fun to be around, but Sherry enjoyed her job and knew that she had to take the good with the bad. She didn't know whether Mrs Alderson had always been like this or if she had got worse since having limited mobility. She knew she was a spinster, but she didn't pry into the whys and whatnots with her. They didn't share an open friendly relationship, theirs was more of a professional one. And Sherry was happy to keep it that way.

She closed the front door behind her and walked up the hallway which had been blandly decorated with magnolia matt emulsion, on the walls and on the ceiling. She stepped lightly over the green, deep pile carpet and headed towards the lounge, taking care not to step off the protective runner that ran the full length. There was a set of three small oil paintings on the right-hand wall and each one showing a different Cornish cottage; the sort you used to find adorning the lid of a box of chocolates. Sherry pushed open the lounge door and found Mrs Alderson sitting in her favourite chair, watching the TV. Her care requirements were different to those of Mrs Johnson and Sherry was only there to cook and clean for her and to do any necessary laundry.

"Good morning, how are you today?" Sherry enquired, almost business-like.

"Not too bad, thank you, Sherry. I had to call the doctor last night. I had a bad headache, and well you know, at my age you can never be too careful. I didn't want to find out too late that I was having a stroke or a brain haemorrhage. As it turned out he told me to take two Paracetamol and I felt a lot better within half an hour. Although I have got quite a lot of lower back pain today and my right knee is slightly swollen, which could be an early indication of water retention, so I may have to call him again later."

Sherry rolled her eyes for the second time since she'd arrived. She had realised early on in their relationship that Mrs Alderson was a hypochondriac and an attention seeker. She seemed to enjoy sharing, in great length, the grim details of her supposed ailments.

"Oh dear. Well, I am glad your headache has gone. Now what would you like for your lunch today?" Sherry asked, swiftly steering the subject in a different direction.

"There's a piece of salmon in the fridge. I'll have it with a few boiled potatoes and broccoli please, dear;" she replied.

"Okay, no problem. I'll be in the kitchen if you need me: Would you like anything to drink?"

"Hmm, yes, I'll have a glass of the sweet white wine that's chilling in the fridge."

"Okey-dokey," Sherry said as she thought that the amount of wine Mrs Alderson drank probably had far more to do with her headache than a brain haemorrhage. Sherry thought about Mrs Johnson, and she smiled to herself as the words 'chalk and cheese' sprang to mind.

After lunch had been cooked, served, and eaten, Sherry put the dishes into the dish washer and loaded up the washing machine, she switched it on to a short programme and vacuumed and cleaned. Once the washer had finished, she transferred the wet washing from the machine on to the clothes horse to dry overnight and then went back into the lounge where Mrs Alderson was watching the news.

"Is there anything else you need me to do before I go?" she asked.

"Hark a minute, dear, I'm just listening to this on the news," she said, keeping her eyes on the screen: "There's been no progress in finding the killer of the two women that were murdered in the woods." She looked over to where Sherry was standing. "You know it's not safe anywhere these days. That's two murders in as many months. You must be careful and mind yourself now. Keep away from these parks and wooded places. It must have been awful for those poor girls. Heaven knows what they must have gone through before they… well, you know."

Sherry nodded her agreement and said: "I know. It doesn't bear thinking about. I can't even begin to imagine how terrifying it must have been." Sherry's voice was overflowing with compassion. "But you don't need to worry about me, I rarely go out at night on my own, and I definitely do not go jogging! I've finished now so if there's nothing else, I'll see you at the same time tomorrow."

"All right, dear. Thank you," She was already looking back at the TV, "bye, love."

Sherry closed the front door firmly behind her and pushed on it to make sure that it had locked.

That was the first time Mrs Alderson had ever shown her any form of concern.

She likes me, she smiled to herself as she got into her car.

CHAPTER SEVEN

As the frost glistened on the ground the full moon lit up the sky. Even though it was the middle of winter and dark, it never ceased to amaze me just how much you could see by the light of the moon. I was parked on the edge of Hinton Wood, which was roughly half an hour's drive away from the village where I lived. I had chosen wisely when I purchased my house; its location was quite central to all the local parks and woodland. Right now, I felt like a cat sitting by a mouse-hole, not daring to move, as it waited patiently for its prey to come out. I was ready to pounce.

My last hunting trip had been a total disaster. Although I had succeeded in taking her life, it was messy and that was not my style. It had been my own stupid fault because I'd been driven by anger and lost control of my emotions, so tonight I needed to be more careful and avoid making a similar mistake. My spine tingled at the thought of killing someone. Well, obviously, not just anyone, a privileged one.

Timing was paramount at this time of year, because during the winter months, people didn't go out so late. Luckily for me, some did still make the effort! That's what I liked about athletic people, they were dedicated to their cause.

A bit like me.

I lit up a cigarette and breathed in the smoke allowing the nicotine to gush around my body, making me feel lightheaded. I could see a woman in my wing mirror, jogging towards my car. As she passed by, she turned her head and looked directly at me and for a split second our eyes locked together. She looked momentarily troubled, so I smiled at her. This had the desired effect and seemed to relax and reassure her. Most probably because she could see it was a woman sitting in the car. I watched the dancing lights that flashed from her hi-tech trainers as she continued running.

I sat there for a few minutes and finished my cigarette. I found myself wondering how people could be so stupid. I mean, come on! Jogging down a country lane, surrounded by nothing but woodland is just asking for trouble, especially when it has been plastered all over the news that there is a murderer on the loose. They really should know better than to be out on their own in the dark.

"Silly bitch," I growled, beginning to feel angry with this woman. She deserved what was coming to her. Because she, of all people, should know better. She was supposed to be an intelligent individual. After all, that is why she's on my list in the first place.

I got out of the car, and, with a black bag tucked under my arm, I ran off up the lane.

I had to jog quite quickly to catch up with her and as I began to close the gap between us, she must have sensed that someone was there because she looked back to see who was coming up behind her. The look on her face was one of relief when she saw that it was me.

"Hi," I said, then I smiled at her. "I hope you don't mind me catching you up, only I'm a bit nervous on my own. I was in two minds whether to come out at all, you know, with what's been reported on the news lately. So, if it's okay with you, it makes me feel safer to jog with someone."

"No, I don't mind. To be honest, I would be glad of your company. I don't generally run on my own either, especially in the dark, but I've had to over the last few weeks because my friend's knee gave out on her and she has been told to rest it, so, here I am!"

Much to my dismay she felt the need to explain herself further:

"I'm on a strict training plan and I didn't want to mess it up, so I thought what the hell, ten minutes won't hurt, but that was already half an hour ago!" She laughed, then repeated herself: "It's great to have some company. I'm Kim!"

I refrained from saying; 'I know who you are,' and instead said, "Nice to meet you," without offering my name.

The good thing about jogging is that you don't have to chat much along the way, so we ran in relative silence and concentrated more on our breathing than on conversing, which suited me fine. I don't normally take the time to get to know my victims before I kill them. After about half a mile we turned off left, into the woodland. This would complete the last leg of our journey together and unbeknown to Kim, the last leg of her life. I smiled as a thrill of excitement zipped down my spine.

"What's with the black bag?" Kim asked, panting slightly.

"Oh," I said, "I wear it if it rains, I hate getting wet."

She laughed at me, and we continued up a slight incline.

A few paces on and without any warning I caught my foot on something and tripped over. "Damn!" I cried out as I landed heavily.

Kim stopped in her tracks and turned to face me. "Are you okay?" she asked, as she rushed to my aid.

"I'm not sure," I lied, as I tried to stand up and winced loudly from the fake agonising pain in my leg.

Kim was quick to put her arm around my shoulders to steady me. "Hold onto me." She said.

How sweet.

"Thanks. I've probably got something in here that I can use as a support," I said, as I unrolled my black bag and took out a chiffon scarf. As I ran my fingers over the silky fabric I shuddered with pleasure. But before I had a chance to use it, I was brought back to reality by two male joggers who suddenly appeared from nowhere. Startled by the surprise company, I hastily shoved the scarf back into the bag before anyone could see it.

The two men stopped when they saw us. "Are you okay?" they asked. "Do you need any help?"

"I'm not sure," Kim said, as she looked at me for the answer, "Do we?"

"No, I don't think so. Thanks though," I said, smiling weakly. "It's nothing serious. I'll be fine. I just tripped over something and jarred my knee, that's all."

Unfortunately for me, those two good Samaritans insisted on walking us all the way back to my car. I thanked them for their kind offer and smiled at them through gritted teeth, which I think they mistook for pain. I managed to convince them that I was okay to drive. I thanked them again for their kindness and got into the driving seat.

An overwhelming feeling of disappointment swept over me as I realised that my research had gone to waste. I watched as Kim and the two men jogged off together and disappeared into the darkness before starting the engine.

"Fuck. That was close!"

CHAPTER EIGHT

Sherry hadn't seen the weather forecast the night before and consequently she had been caught out by the arrival of a heavy frost. Her car windscreen was frozen, and she had forgotten to buy a can of de-icer. Her time was precious in the morning and even a ten-minute delay could make a huge difference to the amount of traffic she would meet on her journey. Although it was tempting to pour a kettle of hot water over the frozen windscreen, she didn't want to run the risk of cracking it, so instead she chose to scrape it. She sighed as she began the arduous task of clearing the windscreen and side windows. She had started the engine and left it running so the heater was already working to remove the ice from the rear window. Satisfied with her efforts, she went back indoors and picked up her hot mug of tea. She cupped her frozen fingers around it, and they tingled as they began to warm up.

She walked over to where the cat was curled up on the sofa. "Well, Thomas, it might look pretty out there but I have to say, I could definitely live without frost." He lifted his head, and she tickled him under his chin. "I'd stay right here if I were you."

She finished her tea, locked the door behind her and got into her car. She hated driving in the rush hour at the best of times, so driving in heavy frost and heavy traffic, was just going to be a joy: It seemed that other commuters, unlike herself, were oblivious to the icy driving conditions and were still rushing to be somewhere, driving carelessly, so as not to be late.

Fifteen minutes or so into her journey the traffic in front of her suddenly ground to a halt. She couldn't see what the hold-up was, but the jam looked like it was going nowhere fast.

Oh great! I wonder what's happened.

She reached over to the dashboard to turn on the radio and pressed the pre-tuned buttons until she found the local station, her shoulders slumped, and she let out a sigh as the breaking news was reported. There was a road traffic accident on the B54, and it had given the police cause to close the road and all the traffic was being diverted around the outskirts of town.

Oh crap, that's me then. She sighed heavily. *I am going to be late. Still, better to be stuck in traffic than smashed up in an accident.*

Her thoughts turned to Mrs Johnson. Sherry knew that as soon as it went past 9 a.m., she would start to fret, but there was nothing she could do about it.

Forty-five minutes later, Sherry pulled up outside Mrs Johnson's house. She got out of the car and tried to run, but she almost slipped over on the frosty pavement. She steadied herself and managed to avoid a collision with the paving slabs and walked with a lot more care up the pathway towards the front door. As she tried to put the key in the lock, she noticed it was already open. With a sinking feeling in her stomach, she pushed open the door and called out, "Hi, Mrs Johnson, it's me, Sherry, are you all, right? I'm coming in!"

But no cheery voice called back to her.

Nothing but an eerie silence greeted her, and this unnerved her even more. Mixed emotions of being scared but duty bound escalated through her as she picked her way cautiously down the hallway towards the downstairs bedroom. Everything looked normal so far and as Sherry stopped in the doorway, she fought back the urge to be sick. Haunting thoughts were trying to push their way forward to the front of her mind; they seemed to be reminiscent of a day from a long time ago and as she battled to force her mind back to the present, she had a really bad feeling.

She took in a deep breath and pushed the bedroom door open. Her eyes were met with ransacked items that were strewn across the floor and then she saw Mrs Johnson lay half in and half out of bed!

"Oh my God!" Sherry's own fear was instantly forgotten as her hand hunted in her pocket for her mobile phone. She pulled it out and dialled 999 whilst rushing over to the bedside to take hold of Mrs Johnson's hand. It was cold but there was a faint pulse.

"Emergency services, what service do you require?" a male voice asked.

"I need an ambulance please. No, Police. No, oh God, I need both. For Mrs Johnson, at 27 Appleby Close, Hinton, H15 2BQ and please hurry!" Sherry pleaded.

The male voice responded with a question: "What's your name, caller?"

"What do you mean, what's my name? For God's sake, just send an ambulance. She's been attacked, she's eighty-seven years old and you want to waste precious time taking my name?"

"I'm going to need you to calm down, caller. I have ordered an ambulance and it is already on the way to you. It will be at the address you have given me within five minutes. So can I take your name please?"

"Oh. Thank you," Sherry's shoulders slumped. "I'm sorry," she said with tears tumbling down her cheeks. "I didn't mean to be rude, it's just so awful." She began to describe what she could see: "Drawers and cupboards are open, and her personal things are all over the floor." She took in a deep breath and continued to answer the question. "My name is Sherry Taylor and I'm Mrs Johnson's carer. I've just got here, and I found her like this. I was late today, there was an accident on the B54, and I was held up and maybe if I hadn't been… Oh, this could all be my fault!" Sherry sobbed into the phone. "I knew something was wrong because the front door was open."

"Okay, try to breathe slowly, deep breaths now, and let's try and keep you calm. I don't want to alarm you but is there a chance that the intruder is still in the property?" the operator asked in a sombre voice.

"Oh my God," Sherry jumped as fear bled through her and she spun round with her eyes fixated on the door: "I never thought to check. What if he is? What if whoever did this is still here?" Her heart felt like it was beating in her throat.

"Do you want me to stay on the line with you, Sherry?" The voice on the end of the phone was gentle.

"Yes please," Sherry replied as more tears streamed down her face.

"Okay, try to remain calm. I will stay on the line with you until the ambulance arrives. So how is Mrs Johnson doing?"

Sherry knelt down on the floor and took hold of her beloved friend's hand. "She's really cold, but she is breathing. I want to move her back into a comfortable position, but I know that's not advisable. I hate to see her lying here like this, half in and half out of her bed. I can't imagine who would do something so awful to such a lovely lady. I've just placed a pillow at the side of her head, and I've pulled her duvet over her, I hope that's okay." And then Sherry began to shake as sobs racked through her body.

She could hear the sirens screaming out as the police and the ambulance both arrived at the same time. She thanked the man on the end of the phone and disconnected the call.

While the paramedics were attending to Mrs Johnson, a young Police officer tried to comfort Sherry.

"Are you Miss Taylor?" he asked.

Sherry nodded her response.

"Come on," the young Officer said, "there's nothing more you can do for her. Come with me, she's in the best hands now. Do you want me to call someone for you?"

"No, there's no one, I'll be okay. It's just such a terrible shock!"

She felt very vulnerable standing there with tears on her cheeks and as she turned to follow the officer, she rummaged through her pockets for a tissue. The Policeman took her outside and over to the incident support vehicle that had also arrived and was parked on the opposite side of the road. He led her inside the vehicle which resembled a motor home, with chairs inside and a kitchenette. He seated her down and handed her a steaming hot cup of sweet tea.

"I'm Sergeant Steve Wallis" he said, "and I need to ask you if you have touched anything inside the house this morning?" His voice had a soothing effect on Sherry.

"No nothing, I just held her hand."

"Okay, that's good, I know this is a difficult time, but I need to ask you some questions, can we do that now or would you rather leave it until later?"

"No, let's do it now while it's fresh in my mind."

She answered his questions as best she could as she sipped her tea. It had a vile taste of sugar, but the hot drink did something to comfort her.

"Where have they taken her to?"

"Hinton General, I would imagine, but I will check that for you."

Sherry looked up at him with sadness in her eyes and said, "She hasn't got any family, do you think the hospital staff will be able to tell me how she is, with me not being a relative?"

"Don't worry; I will make sure they know the situation and that you are her Carer. Would you like me to drive you home?"

Sherry shook her head as she put her half-empty tea mug down and stood up. "No thank you, I'll be fine, my car's outside. Is it okay for me to go now?"

"Yes, but are you sure you feel up to driving?"

Sherry could hear the genuine concern in his voice, and she nodded.

"Someone may contact you again," he said as he handed her a card with his details on.

Sherry looked at it and read the name, Sergeant Wallis. She thanked him for his kindness and put the card into her pocket.

She drove home, oblivious to the traffic jams and holdups that had delayed her journey earlier that morning.

She turned the key and pushed open her own front door, and Thomas twitched an ear and looked up as she sat next to him on the sofa. She snuggled him to her and sat there in disbelief.

CHAPTER NINE

Detective Sergeant Rob Wilding was sitting with his feet up on the desk, reading through a new case file that he had been handed upon his arrival at work that morning. Dropping the file onto the desk he stretched as he looked at his watch. He jumped to his feet and swiftly headed out of the office in the direction of the coffee machine. "Morning, Sophie," he said and smiled at the cleaning lady.

"Morning Rob," Sophie smiled back as she pushed her glasses up onto the top of her head. "Is it that time already?"

"Yep, its eight twenty-five and any minute now he will walk through that door and expect his caffeine fix to be on his desk!"

They both laughed, Rob liked Sophie, but he had no time to chat this morning. In fact, he barely had enough time to get the coffee back to the office and put the steaming hot cup down on Strain's desk before he walked in: "Alright Guv?"

"Yes, thanks Rob," Strain replied. "What's new?"

"An elderly lady has died in Hinton. It appears to be as a result of a botched burglary. So, I guess that makes it a homicide or manslaughter. Whichever it is, it's another one for us." He sighed as he looked over at the incident board. He had already updated it with all the information that they had on the new case.

"Have you got the address?" Strain asked as he picked up his coffee.

"It's all in here," Rob said as he handed over the file.

Strain took it from him and briefly read through the paperwork it contained.

He stood up: "Come on then, let's go." He swigged down the last mouthful of his coffee, tucked the file under his arm and they both left the office.

The journey to twenty-seven, Appleby Close was achieved in relative silence. Friendly chit chat did not flow comfortably between them yet, but Rob was eager for an update on Strain's personal life and was trying to think how he might broach the subject. "So did you go to the Pub last night, Guv?" he asked in a casual manner.

"Yes, I did, it was a good night. You should have come along."

By the time they arrived at the crime scene the forensic team were already hard at work in every room. They both stopped at the front door and slipped on a pair of shoe covers and gloves that were handed to them by a young PC.

"Remind me again, who was it that found her? Was it a Sherry Tyler?" Strain asked, he knew of course, but he was testing Rob, to see how much information he had absorbed from the file.

"Sherry Taylor, she's the carer. The old lady was alive then..."

"Show some respect please, Rob. Has this old lady got a name?"

"Yes Guv. Sorry." He cleared his throat. "Mrs Johnson was initially found alive, but she died a few hours later, in hospital. Unfortunately, she never regained consciousness. They reckon it was heart failure from the shock."

"Do we know what was taken?"

"Well according to the carer, on the report from the officer who was first on the scene, it didn't look like there was anything missing, as far as she could tell anyway. In fact, none of the other rooms had been tampered with, only the bedroom. That's strange, right?"

"Maybe they were disturbed, or they did a runner when Mrs Johnson had a turn. Okay, let's get on with the usual; canvas the area, knock on some doors. Interview the neighbours, see if any of them saw or heard anything. And talk to the carer. We want the names of everyone with a key to the property. Have her family been notified yet?"

"Apparently, she doesn't have any family. Her husband died thirty years ago and there aren't any other living relatives."

"Right. If you need me, I'll be at Hinton General. I need to speak to the pathologist. I'll take the car."

"I'll just catch a bus back then, shall I?" Rob whined.

"I'm sure uniform will give you a lift back to the station if you ask them nicely," he said, and then disappeared out of the front door.

CHAPTER TEN

During the journey over to the hospital, Strain's thoughts drifted back to his date. He didn't feel comfortable talking to Rob about Christie, so he had kept it to himself, but she had been good company and great in bed too. It had been the best sex he'd had in a long time. His night of passion had left him feeling good and he hoped they would see each other again. He wasn't sure how that would happen though, as she had left without leaving her phone number.

Strain entered the hospital through the main entrance and passed his hands under the sanitizer dispenser. As he rubbed the clear gel in, he took the lift down to the lower ground floor. This was where the mortuary and the pathology labs were located. He hadn't been here since escorting the grief-stricken parents of Jenna Hopkins, who was the last victim in his ongoing case, to view their daughter. He thought back to that day and how you had to be made of steel to witness the overwhelming grief of parents when they came to identify one of their children. And as if that wasn't bad enough, he then had to tell them that her body was being transferred and would need to be held until the coroner had conducted a post-mortem examination and concluded an accurate cause of death. Dealing with death was bad enough but having to deal with living relatives was definitely one of the more unpleasant parts of his job.

He walked briskly down the corridor and could smell the crisp sterile air intensify as he approached the pathology lab. He pushed on the swing doors, and he could see the pathologist standing over a corpse at the far end of the room. After a brief nod of acknowledgement had passed between them, the pathologist beckoned to Strain to join him, he did as he was asked and positioned himself on the opposite side of the table so that he was facing him. He looked down at Mrs Johnson's dead body and listened as the pathologist went on to confirm what Rob had said earlier:

"There are no signs of a physical attack and no broken bones, and there isn't any visible bruising. This poor soul suffered a fatal cardiac arrest, which was more than likely caused by the high anxiety levels that she would have experienced by having an intruder in her home." He looked over the top of his glasses at Strain and waited for his comments.

Satisfied with this information, Strain nodded. "Okay, then. I don't see any point in transferring her body over to our own lab for a forensic examination. I'll be in touch," he said as he turned and left the room.

He drove back to the station, grabbed a coffee from the machine and sat down at his desk. Rob arrived back a short while later and informed him that although each resident in the Close had been interviewed, no one had recalled seeing anything out of the ordinary on the particular evening in question. Forensics had found a large sum of money and jewellery that could quite easily have been found but had not been stolen, so they concluded that her room had been ransacked more out of anger than a hunt for any valuables, which didn't make any sense, because there always had to be a motive.

"It wasn't even a forced entry," Rob said. "Looks like the intruder had a key. I haven't spoken to the carer yet. Apparently, she has gone into delayed shock and her doctor has had to sedate her. I'll talk to her as soon as she is ready."

"Have you tried calling the agency that she works for, because they will have a list of all the people who currently hold a key?"

"I haven't, Guv. I'll do that now."

CHAPTER ELEVEN

Sherry opened her eyes. They were sensitive and painfully sore from the constant flow of her tears and as she tried to focus, she could feel her head pounding. Her thoughts were trapped in the moment when she had called the hospital on the evening of that tragic day. Over and over, she had relived it, unable to get the conversation out of her head. She had not been anywhere close to being prepared for them to tell her such terrible news. The thought had not entered her head that Mrs Johnson might actually die, and she couldn't believe it when they had told her that she had. In fact, initially, she had refused to believe what they were telling her and had accused them of lying. She had called back and spoken to a different person who had sadly conveyed the same heart-breaking news to her. This was the precise moment that her meltdown had started. Recognising that this tragic event may be bigger than she would be able to cope with on her own, she had called her doctor, who consequently had made a home visit and given her a small amount of sedation, just enough to calm her down. As a result, Sherry had slept soundly.

    She had stayed at home for the next three days. She felt safe tucked away under her duvet. On the fourth morning, although far from being over the loss of Mrs Johnson, she at least felt well enough to get up. She checked her phone and found that there were seven messages left on her voicemail from a Sergeant Rob Wilding. She played them back, one by one. They all said virtually the same thing, which was that he urgently needed to speak with her to clarify some details regarding the late Mrs Johnson.

She was horrified. She didn't want to talk about it, not to anyone, not now or ever. It was the worst thing she had ever had to deal with in her life. But she also knew that he wouldn't leave her alone until he had spoken to her, so she called the number he had left for her, and between them they arranged for him to come to her house rather than have Sherry make the journey to the station in town. But wherever the interview was going to take place, Sherry knew it was going to be difficult and she wasn't sure how she would get through answering his questions. Regardless, the appointment was made for half past ten the following morning. Sherry felt relieved because this meant that at the very least, she had all afternoon and the rest of the night to mentally prepare for it.

CHAPTER TWELVE

Rob was pleased to finally get a call from Sherry Taylor and when he went to see her at her home, he was very gentle with her, he was somewhat distracted though. She was an attractive woman, with long, golden-blonde hair and eyes that were the colour of an icy blue lake. Although they were slightly bloodshot, presumably from all the recent upset. She was around five foot eight and a slim size ten, possibly in her early thirties. He hoped that he would be looked after by someone like her when he was old and needy. The long-awaited interview was, however, fruitless, as Sherry couldn't offer any more information to Rob than he already had. As far as she knew, she was the only one who had a key.

"I'm really sorry for your loss," Rob said to her, sincerely. "It seems like you were very close to her."

"Thank you, and yes, we were very close, she was a special lady," Sherry said, squeezing the tissue in her hand.

As Rob got to his feet, he felt something on his leg, and he looked down to find a cat furring around his ankle. "Hello, you" he said, as he bent down to stroke him.

"Thomas, come here," she clicked her fingers at the cat. "Sorry Sergeant"

"No worries" Rob said, as he continued to stroke him, "I've been thinking of getting a cat for myself." He stood upright and said: "Thank you for your time, Miss Taylor. That's all for now, but I'm sorry to say that I am going to need you to pop down to the station so that we can take a copy of your fingerprints, and then we can eliminate you from our enquires."

Sherry's eyes filled up with tears and she nodded. "Yes of course, it's just another thing to do that makes this whole nightmare real." She stood up and walked towards the front door. "Shall I come in this afternoon?"

"That would be great if you don't mind. I could send a car to pick you up at around two o clock if that's any good?"

"Thank you. That would be helpful," Sherry agreed.

Once again Rob thanked her for her time and co-operation and left her with his card in case she had any further information for him. She took it from him and glanced at it before dropping it onto the coffee table along with the other card that Sergeant Wallis had given her.

As she closed the door behind him, she caught sight of herself in the mirror that was hanging on the lounge wall. She was already a shadow of the person she had been five days ago; her eyes were bloodshot, and she had dark circles underneath them.

She sighed heavily.

I look like something out of a horror film.

She went into the bathroom and rummaged through her cosmetic draw until she found a pack of cool cucumber eye pads and took them into the bedroom, where she lay on the bed and placed a pad on each eye and tried to relax as she thought about her best friend, Tracy.

It had been too long since she had seen her, and she wished that she was here now. They had been friends since nursery school and Sherry longed to feel the comfort of her friend's arms around her, but instead, here, she was all alone, surrounded by the emptiness of her new world and as if he felt her loneliness, Thomas nudged her arm and curled up by her side, Sherry stroked him, grateful for his affection.

For a moment she let herself think about her work. The agency that employed her had been kind and had made alternative arrangements for the care of Mrs Alderson. They had told her to take as much time off as she needed to recover from this terrible tragedy. Sherry didn't think she would ever recover.

CHAPTER THIRTEEN

As promised, the police car arrived to collect Sherry at 2 p.m. and took her to the main police Station in town. The procedure for finger printing didn't take very long but the paperwork seemed to take forever to complete, in fact, it took a little over an hour and a half. As she stepped out of the lift and walked towards the first door leading to the exit, she became aware that the door was being held open for her and she quickened her pace so as not to keep him waiting. She looked up to thank the person who was holding it.

"Christie!" Strain said, a lot louder than he meant to.

Sherry looked behind her and then back at Strain. "Who me? I'm sorry, you must be mistaken."

He laughed. "Well, you must have a double then, they say everybody has one – but I'm sorry, I didn't mean to startle you."

Sherry managed a weak smile and walked away from him, pushing through another door down the corridor that would lead her out of the building. Strain shook his head as he watched her leave. He walked into the office to find Rob sitting at his desk doing paperwork.

"Who was the young lady I just passed in the corridor?" Strain asked Rob, as he sat down at his own desk.

"That was Sherry Taylor, the carer I told you about."

"She's an absolute ringer for Christie, the girl I met in the pub the other night."

"Maybe they're sisters!"

"No, I don't think so, I just called her Christie and she looked totally blank."

Seemingly satisfied that it wasn't Christie, Strain dismissed any further thoughts and turned his attention to the four-o-clock meeting he had scheduled for a progress update on their current cases. As the remainder of his team filed into his office he picked up what he needed from his desk and stood in front of the incident board and he faced his audience, who immediately quietened down as he began to speak.

"Right, this is what we've got, people? Two murdered joggers: A Mrs Anne Holland who was strangled to death and a Miss Jenna Hopkins who was beaten to death. These two young women lost their lives within the last two months and both are seemingly unrelated. However, it is our belief that they were killed by the same person. The similarity lies with the chiffon scarf that was placed over both of their faces and to date this information has not been made public knowledge, so let's keep it that way for now please. Unfortunately, we now have another incident to investigate: Mrs Johnson, who died of a cardiac arrest, possibly resulting from being frightened to death due to a burglary gone wrong. Obviously, I don't think for one minute that these murder cases are related to the robbery, but then you never know; weirder things have been known to happen. And that's what we are here to find out. So has anybody got anything useful to add?" Strain's eyes scanned the room and a fidgety silence filled the office. "No, well, get out there and find something. Run more background checks on the two women, find me a link. Interview the neighbours again at Appleby close. Someone has got to have seen or heard something, but they just don't know it."

"But Guv," said a young PC who was standing at the back of the room. "Regarding Mrs Johnson, the immediate neighbours have all said the same thing, and that is, they only saw one person entering the property on the night in question and that was the carer, err…" forgetting for a moment that the information had already been updated on the incident board behind Strain, he quickly shuffled through his paperwork to check his notes, "... Sherry Taylor. She goes twice a day every day and has done for the last year."

"Well, clearly, there is a piece of information missing, something that somebody doesn't realise is important. Do we have an exact time for her second visit?"

"Yes Guv," said the same young PC, "she goes at four thirty pm to do the old dear her dinner!"

"So, what time did she leave? Speak to her again and the neighbours. They've all had some time to think it through now, and we need answers. Okay? I want you to go through every piece of forensic on the two murdered joggers and find me that link. There has to be one. There is always a motive."

As he looked around the room he threw his hands up in the air and said in a slightly raised voice: "What are you waiting for? This case isn't going to solve itself!"

The office emptied as his team speedily scurried off in different directions.

CHAPTER FOURTEEN

It was late evening by the time Rob pulled up outside Mrs Johnson's house. He was going to interview her immediate neighbour. He knocked on the door of number twenty-five and an elderly lady opened it. She was wearing a pair of tweed trousers and a thick woollen cardigan with a blouse underneath it that was buttoned right up to her neck. Rob thought she might be in her mid to late sixties.

"Mrs Burrows?" he asked.

"Yes, can I help you?" She looked at him with a quizzical eye.

"Mrs Burrows, my name is Sergeant Wilding," and he held out his ID card.

She took it from him and studied it carefully.

"Would it be okay for me to come in and ask you a few questions regarding your neighbour, Mrs Johnson?" Rob asked politely.

"Yes, of course," she said handing him back his ID card. "Come in, but I'm not sure I can be of any help to you. I have already told the police everything I know."

Rob followed her along the neatly kept hallway and through a door on the right that opened into the lounge. It was decorated in a distinct seventies style, with a wall to wall fitted green carpet. She gestured towards a floral-patterned sofa for him to sit down. He imagined his own grandmother would have had a similar taste in decor if she had still been alive.

"Would you like a cup of tea, Sergeant?"

"Er, go on then, thank you," he said and then added, "Milk, no sugar."

She came back in with a tray of tea and biscuits and set it down on the coffee table in front of Rob, he picked up the cup closest to him and she offered him the plate of biscuits.

"Lovely, thank you," Rob said, as he took a chocolate one. "Have you lived here long?"

"Almost twelve years. My husband and I moved here hoping to enjoy our retirement together, we had always loved the New Forest, but sadly he passed away quite suddenly, three years ago."

"I'm sorry to hear that," Rob said sincerely. He finished his biscuit and washed it down with a mouthful of tea. "What can you tell me about the day of the incident involving Mrs Johnson?"

"Not much really, I saw Sherry, that's Edna's carer, at about nine o clock in the morning and she left about eleven. Then she came back at 4.30, to do Edna's dinner, and that's about it really. Those were her regular visiting times, everyday, seven days a week. She has been looking after Edna for about a year now. Such a lovely girl, young Sherry, so kind and helpful. Edna adored her. I didn't see anyone else all day except the postman, oh and number thirty-one had a delivery from Parcel Quick. A big box, I can't imagine what was in it!"

Rob smiled to himself at the accurate observations that Mrs Burrows had unknowingly made.

"I did see Sherry again later that night when I let Mr Baggins in. That's my cat. It must have been about 8.15. I'm not sure whether she was coming or going but I remember the time because it was the advert break in my programme."

Rob made a few notes, but she hadn't told him anything that he didn't already know. He finished his tea and stood up. "Thank you for your time, Mrs Burrows. We'll be in touch if there's anything else we need to ask you, and thanks again for the tea."

"You're very welcome," she said, as she followed Rob down the hallway to the front door. "I hope you find whoever did this, Sergeant."

As he stepped outside, he turned to face her. "I can assure you we will," he said, sounding a lot more confident than he actually felt.

CHAPTER FIFTEEN

Sherry woke up in a hot sweat, panting and gasping for air. By shaking her head furiously, she had managed to escape from her nightmare. She had been dreaming that she was inside Mrs Johnson's house, actually in there with her when the intruder had opened the front door and walked down the corridor to where Sherry was standing. She couldn't see a face, but it was obvious to Sherry that the intruder knew exactly where they were going, they had clearly been there before.

With fear rising to her throat, she reached for the bedside lamp and switched it on. Her bedroom lit up and she let out a short sharp scream, "Oh my God, Tracy, you made me jump. What are you doing here?" Without waiting for an answer, she scrambled out of bed and almost launched herself into her friend's arms to give her a hug. "I am so pleased to see you." Sherry was crying now, "I've had the most awful time lately, hold me tight." Tracy did as she was told and held her friend in her arms and comforted her as she cried. After a while, Sherry pulled away from her and she could smell a mixture of perfume and alcohol on her friends' clothes as she sat down on the bed. "I can't believe you're here," she said as she dabbed at her eyes with the tissue Tracy had given her, and with a feeble smile she said, "I must look a right mess. You look nice though, have you been out somewhere?" Sherry gave her a disapproving look.

But Tracy just smiled at her.

"How did you get in anyway?"

"You gave me a key, remember?" Tracy replied calmly.

"No, I don't remember." Sherry felt jealous that her friend had obviously been out having a good time, while she had been here on her own, going through hell. And this knowledge made her feel mildly irritated "You know I love you, but I wish you wouldn't just let yourself into my home whenever the fancy takes you." Sherry reached out for her friend's hand and squeezed it affectionately, her mood softening slightly. "You scared me. I was only thinking about you earlier, and I have been looking forward to seeing you, but not like this, maybe you should leave now, you've obviously been drinking." Sherry's heart was racing as she studied her friend and she wanted to hug her again, but something didn't feel right. She detected the air of calm that seemed to embrace Tracy a few minutes ago had now evaporated and was clearly replaced with despair:

"Sherry, listen to me please, I need you to forgive me, you have to," Tracy begged.

Sherry snatched her hand back, "What do you mean 'forgive you'? What have you done?" She watched as her friends' eyes filled with tears and she let out a gasp as her hand flew to her mouth. "No! Was it you? Please, tell me it wasn't you!" Sherry bought her knees up and hugged them to her. Her shoulders slumped down. "Is that why you haven't been to see me? Because you killed my friend?" I thought you had changed. You promised me you had changed." Sherry looked her in the eye. "Give me one good reason why you think I should ever forgive you?" Sherry's voice was quieter now. "Why did you do it?"

Tracy sat down next to Sherry on the edge of the bed. "I don't know why, I mean, I didn't kill her, I didn't want her to die, it just happened. If only I hadn't gone there, everything would still be the same. She wouldn't be dead, and you wouldn't hate me!"

"Hate is not the right word," Sherry said. "I could never hate you. I love you; I just don't understand you. We grew up together, we did everything, together, but I just don't get you anymore and now you have taken someone very precious away from me." She took in a long breath and then said, "We need to call the police."

Tracy's face crumpled. "Please don't. They'll never believe that it was an accident, and I'll end up in prison."

Sherry looked down at her hands; they felt sweaty as she twisted them together. "I need some time to think. You had better go now or I might say something I'll regret."

"I can't leave, not until I know that you forgive me. It was a stupid accident, please believe me, I can't go on without you. You are everything to me; I need you in my life."

Sherry stared at the beautiful young woman who was sitting in front of her and with an over whelming feeling of sadness she lowered her voice to a whisper and said, "Of course I'll forgive you, in time, but you really do need to go now." Sherry watched as Tracy let out a long sigh, she looked relieved, but Sherry also thought she looked surprised with the outcome.

Had Tracy managed to fool her yet again?

She watched as her friend got up, blew Sherry a kiss and left the room.

Sherry waited for a minute or two and then ran down the stairs to her front door, grabbed the handle and breathed a sigh of relief.

It was locked, thank goodness!

She turned and ran to the toilet and threw up, her heart was pounding hard and fast and she leaned back against the wall as she tried to catch her breath. Her thoughts were bouncing around inside her head like the ball in a pin ball machine. She had no idea what she would do with this information. she loved Tracy dearly and she was already regretting taking such a stern attitude with her and was sorry she had told her to leave.

She went into the kitchen and made herself a cup of ginger tea and sat down with it cupped in her hands. She sipped the hot liquid, hoping it would quell the feeling of nausea. She wasn't sure how long she had been sitting there for, but she was starting to feel cold, so she went upstairs and got into bed. Thomas was curled up in the corner of her duvet and as she clicked her fingers and called his name, he obeyed by snuggling up to her.

She stroked him under his chin. "What a mess, Tom," she sighed, and as she lay there listening to him purring, she eventually drifted off to sleep.

CHAPTER SIXTEEN

Sherry wasn't sure how she made it through the next few weeks; they flowed by through a blur of tears. She couldn't find the strength to go back to work and she had spent most of her time sleeping. She was surprised and a little hurt that Tracy hadn't been back in touch. If ever there was a time that she needed her friend, it was now. But Sherry had received no replies to the numerous text messages she had sent to her, so instead, she was struggling alone, finding it difficult to cope with simple everyday tasks. The image of seeing Mrs Johnson like that was etched firmly into her memory and no matter how hard she tried to push it out of her head it remained there like a wound that refused to heal. Her doctor had made the decision to sign her off work and had reluctantly prescribed antidepressants for her. She hadn't wanted to take them at first but that little white tablet, although initially it had made her feel unwell, had now begun to work its magic. At least she could get up in the morning, wash, and dress herself.

A firm of solicitors had contacted her to inform her that, even though the case remained unsolved, the pathologist had released Mrs Johnson's body and they had arranged a service for her cremation as per her wishes, and all too soon the day of her funeral had arrived.

Although the antidepressants were helping Sherry to cope. She had found it difficult getting out of her bed that morning. She was still trying to come to terms with her loss. Maybe she would have been able to accept it better if Mrs Johnson had died from natural causes and not from the fright of an intruder. An intruder that just happened to be her best friend. She knew she should tell the police, but she couldn't bring herself to do it. She was in no state, mentally, to think rational thoughts and she didn't want to lose another person from her life that she loved dearly. Her eyes filled up again as she read a condolence card from Mrs Alderson, who had expressed her sadness. Maybe she wasn't as frosty as Sherry had thought.

She was brought back to reality by a knock on the door. It was the taxi she had ordered. She buttoned up her coat, picked up her gloves and stepped outside into the damp day and climbed into the waiting vehicle.

After a short journey the taxi turned right through an impressive set of gates and began its drive up towards the chapel, it was a beautiful setting, surrounded by its garden of remembrance, but Sherry barely noticed, her stomach was in knots as she dreaded arriving at her destination.

The taxi parked up and she paid the driver, who immediately got out and opened the door for her. As she stepped out and pulled the collar of her coat up around her neck, she walked up the pathway and stood in front of the entrance, repeating to herself; 'you can do this'. She took in a deep breath and went inside the chapel.

An organ was softly playing music, which filled the room, but it was solemn and morose, more of a match for the weather than Mrs Johnson's personality. And for Sherry, this made a sad day even sadder. She looked around at the handful of people that barely filled two rows and saw that Mrs Burrows, who had been Mrs Johnson's neighbour, was one of them.

It's true what they say, you come in on your own and you go out on your own.

She thought of all the people's lives that Mrs Johnson must have touched during her eighty-odd years of existence.

Where were they today?

These thoughts left her with a bitter taste.

Towards the end of the service, during the reading of, 'The Lord is my Shepherd', the coffin began its journey towards the red velvet curtains and Sherry had to hold onto the seat in front of her to steady herself. As she watched it disappear, it felt like a knife was being plunged straight into her heart. She could barely see through her tears. She wanted to run after the coffin and stop it from reaching its destination, but instead she stood there unable to move. Finally with the last prayer read and the service finished the small congregation began to leave the chapel, dropping any small change they had into a collection bowl by the door.

Mrs Burrows came over to where Sherry was standing and hugged her. "Sherry, love, I'm so sorry. It's such a tragedy. If you need anything or you want to chat, you know where to find me."

Sherry looked at her with a mixture of emotions. These kind words did little to comfort her, but it was nice to share a moment with someone else who had known Mrs Johnson. This day had brought to a close a period in Sherry's life that was possibly the happiest she had ever been and now she was left with a huge hole to fill. She had no idea where to go or what to do next. Her immediate future looked bleak and full of sadness and for a second, Sherry desperately wished that Tracy was here with her.

CHAPTER SEVENTEEN

The following week Sherry received a letter from the same Company that had arranged Mrs Johnson's funeral. Barber and May Associates were a well-known firm of solicitors in the small town of Christchurch, about eighteen miles away, and they specialised in family matters. She carefully opened the white envelope and read its contents. It was a request. They wanted to arrange an appointment for her to come into their office and speak with one of their senior partners, a Mr Ermine Sharman. Feeling anxious Sherry rang them and duly arranged a 1 p.m. appointment for the following Thursday afternoon. She raised her fears about why they might want to see her, and the secretary had assured her not to worry as it was regarding the late Mrs Johnson. But Sherry was worried. Why on earth would a solicitor want to see her.

Regardless of her underlying fear, as arranged, the following Thursday found Sherry sitting down opposite Mr Sharman, fidgeting, and twisting her gold signet ring round and round on her finger. She looked at the stark white walls and the dark oak furniture, in a total state of shock, hearing what was being said to her, but not quite able to believe it.

"I'm sorry, but just to be clear, are you telling me that she left me her house?" Sherry said the last five words a lot louder than she meant to.

She sat there quietly for a moment then suddenly she felt a wave of nausea sweep over her, and as she looked around, she could see the office walls were closing in, and as the tears began to flow, she found it increasingly hard to breathe. Agonising breaths felt like they were caught up in a mass of barbed wire in her throat, as the room continued to swish around her. She let out a gasp for air as she reached into her handbag and frantically searched for a brown paper bag. She pulled it out and immediately formed it into a balloon shape and began breathing slowly in, and out, inflating, and deflating it, until the panic attack eased and she could breathe normally again.

Mr Sharman rushed around the desk to her side, but Sherry put her hand up to stop him. After a few moments she composed herself. "Sorry," she murmured, her voice was barely a whisper. "Why would she do such a thing? I've only known her for a year. This has to be a mistake! I knew she had no immediate family, but there must be some distant relative somewhere who would surely be more entitled to her estate than I am."

As Mr Sharman sat back down at his desk, Sherry could see he was shaken up by what he had just witnessed, but he remained calm and professional as he spoke. "I can assure you, Miss Taylor, there is no mistake. Mrs Johnson was of a sound mind, and she was very specific with her instructions regarding her will. She also left a sum of money for you."

Sherry sat there with tears trickling down her cheeks as she once again rifled through her handbag, this time for a tissue.

"Are you sure you are all right, Miss Taylor. Would you like a glass of water? Is there anyone I can call for you?"

Sherry shook her head. "No, there's no one, I'll be fine." As she got up to leave his office, she smoothed her hands over her skirt.

Mr Sharman also stood up as he said, "I'll be in touch with you as soon as the paperwork for the house is ready for you to sign." He handed her an envelope.

"What's this?" she asked, as she took it from him.

"It's a cheque for £120,000. I suggest you deposit it post haste!"

"Uh...yes, I will, thank you," Sherry stammered. The words stuck in her throat like a piece of dry toast.

She walked out of the office and passed the reception area, she didn't really feel up to driving home yet, so when she came out of the building, she went to the Cafe that she had spotted earlier, just across the road.

She ordered a latte to go and sat in her car and drank the hot, sweet coffee as she tried to make sense of what had just transpired.

During her journey home she was aware of the occasional impatient driver beeping at her, but she didn't care.

Once she was inside her house, she took her mobile out of her handbag and dialled Tracy's number. It rang out five times before switching to voicemail. Sherry was disappointed, but she didn't leave a message for fear of sounding irritated.

She placed her phone onto the kitchen table and picked up the envelope that the solicitor had given her. She ripped it open and took out the cheque.

A smile spread across her face as she read the amount.

CHAPTER EIGHTEEN

Strain and Rob were sitting in the cafeteria eating a full English breakfast together. This was a rare occasion for them, but they classed it as a working breakfast as they discussed their current cases.

"What if the Taylor woman is involved?" Strain said to Rob, before he cleared the last of his food from his plate and washed it down with his mug of tea.

"I think I'd be really surprised to find out that she was, she hardly looks like a murderer."

"What do murderers look like then? Have they got a particular image? Is there a stereotype that I should be on the lookout for?" Strain teased him and laughed. "Okay, then, she isn't a murderer." Strain continued explaining his theory. "Let's say that it was never her intention, but unfortunately that's how it turned out. You said yourself she's the only one with a key and that's by her own admission. Now we find out that she's inherited everything the old lady possessed, her house and her money. It does kind of point the finger right at her and gives her that all important motive."

Rob lifted his shoulder in a half shrug: "You don't seriously believe that do you? I agree that it looks bad, but she adored the woman. She seemed genuinely devastated when she found her."

"I believe what I need to believe to get the job done. So, don't let your judgement get clouded, just because she happens to be a good-looking female."

"It's not clouded by anything" Rob snapped back. "I'm not that shallow, but I really don't think she's involved."

"Well, we can't rule her out at this stage. She's all we've got."

They had both finished eating, so they walked back to the office. "I think you need to pay her another visit and see if you can find out whether she knew that she was going to inherit the old lady's house and money."

Rob managed to resist the urge to say; 'hasn't the old lady got a name, Guv', but he knew being facetious wasn't going to help anything, so instead he left Strain in the office and drove over to Sherry Taylor's house.

Strain pulled his chair out from under the desk and sat down. He put his feet up on the desk and rested his head on his hand. It pissed him off that they didn't have any forensic evidence, in fact they had absolutely jack shit! Chief Superintendent Ridley had had a go at him earlier on and it hadn't been pretty.

"We need answers, and we need to close some cases," he'd all but yelled at Strain.

"Don't you think I know that Sir? With respect, do you think we sit around playing cards all day? My team's out there twelve hours a day, carrying out door-to-door interviews, checking forensics, studying statements, looking for anything that may give us a lead. But we can't move forward without anything to go on and we really don't have anything yet."

"For goodness sake, Strain, calm down, this isn't a personal attack on you! It may surprise you to learn that I too am just another rung in the policing ladder, getting flak from above, and I'm just passing it down. But I think you need some help with this one and it may also surprise you to learn that there are other resources open to us in this very building, so I would like you to involve our resident forensic psychologist, for behaviour analysis. She will be able to provide you with a profile on your murderer."

Strain's face muscles tightened, he was well aware of the woman that the Supt was referring to: "Okay, Sir, I'll sort it. And I do get it. I know it's not a personal attack on me, but unfortunately, sometimes, I do take it personally." Strain turned and left the office and he let out a heavy sigh as he closed the door firmly behind him.

As he recalled their conversation, he had to admit to himself that, in truth, the unsolved crimes weren't the only thing on his mind. That damn woman he'd met a few weeks ago had managed to get right under his skin. Even though he hadn't seen her since that one night, she was never far from his mind and was constantly haunting his thoughts. He flashed back to the day he had held the door open for Sherry Taylor and the uncanny resemblance between them, he wondered if he should be worried about that, he hoped not because he was very keen to see Christie again. He hated not being in control, patience had never been his best asset and he was pissed off that she hadn't been in touch. He cursed himself for not taking her phone number.

CHAPTER NINETEEN

After work Strain and Rob walked to the pub together, but Rob wasn't in the best of moods, so he only stayed for one drink before excusing himself. The reception he had received at Sherry Taylor's house earlier on had bothered him. She had launched a full-scale attack on him, filled with anger, as she'd accused him of thinking that she had something to do with the death of Mrs Johnson. As he walked home his mind churned over the ugly conversation: "Take me in then if you think I did it, go on, why don't you fuck my life up some more? And if that's not the case and you are not going to arrest me, then get the hell out of my house, because this whole business is bad enough without you throwing accusations at me."

Rob had not retaliated as he'd looked at her flushed face and seen the anger brimming over in her eyes, he could see she was on the edge, so instead he let her finish her rant and then he had left feeling sorely bashed and battered and yet he was sorry that she was upset with him. Nevertheless, contrary to his earlier belief, there was a niggling doubt somewhere in the back of his mind that maybe his boss might be right, and Sherry Taylor may well be involved somewhere along the line.

Attack is the best form of defence, and she had certainly done that.

Strain, however, stayed at the pub and ordered another drink and as he took a swig, he heard a familiar voice behind him.

"I could do with a pain killer myself if there's one going?"

His tight features relaxed as he heard her sexy tone, it was like she had pressed a magic button because the effect on him was instant. He couldn't stop the smile that spread over his face as he turned around to face Christie. "And am I correct in assuming that it would be in the form of a Bacardi and coke with ice?"

"Most definitely," she smiled at him. He could see her ice-blue eyes had a look of mischief in them and they played havoc with his insides. He was momentarily transfixed, and it took all his strength not to kiss her right there and then. She looked amazing in a short, fitted dress and a pair of over-the-knee suede boots. Her hair was piled up on top of her head in a messy, sexy style and she wore a light touch of makeup that somehow managed to enhance her good looks.

"You look stunning," Strain said.

"Thank you" she said, as she looked under her eye lashes at him. "Compliments will get you everywhere. You don't look so bad yourself."

Strain got her a drink and they moved away from the bar to a table in the far corner where it was a bit more private. They sat down and Strain tried not to beam too brightly as he asked, "So what have you been up to, stranger?"

She took a sip of her drink and then joked, "Is this an official enquiry?"

He was suddenly glad that he hadn't dived straight in with questions about any look-a-like relatives she may or may not have and said, "Sorry, if that's how it sounded. It's been one of those weeks, but hopefully it just got better."

He could see a wave of sadness wash over her eyes as she spoke.

"Yes, I know what you mean I've had a weird week myself. A friend died recently, and it hit me quite hard, in fact other than to go to work, this is the first time I've ventured out. So how about, no questions. Let's just enjoy ourselves and not talk about anything other than what we are doing right now."

"Sounds good to me" Strain agreed. "Answer me this one thing though; are you married?"

"No, I'm not married."

A wave of relief swept over him: "Excellent news. Now, where were we?"

"We were having a fantastic night together," Christie said, holding up her glass.

CHAPTER TWENTY

Although Rob had only been in this job for six months, he could see that there were a few things in this case that just didn't add up. Unfortunately, his boss, Strain, made his job a lot harder than it needed to be. He wasn't an easy person to talk to and he was extremely unapproachable most of the time. He had an impatient nature and somehow always managed to make Rob feel insignificant. Maybe he didn't mean to, but it left Rob with little or no confidence and unable to share any of his thoughts with him. He hoped, given time this would change and quite frankly, for Rob, the change needed to be sooner rather than later. As he stretched out on his couch with a drink, he picked up the remote control and began flicking through the TV channels.

Four hundred channels and still nothing worth watching.

He sighed as he chucked the remote across onto the other sofa. With no TV to distract him, his mind sifted back through his recent interviews and in particular the one with Mrs Burrows and his thoughts paused at her comment about the night she had seen Sherry Taylor at 8.15. When he had questioned Taylor earlier about the time she had left on that night, she had been adamant that she had left at 7 In fact, the whole conversation was imprinted on his mind:

"It's always 7.00, I don't just come and go to suit myself Sergeant, I have set times to work to. Like I said, I always get there between 4.30 and 5.00 and I leave at 7.00." She had raised her voice at him. "Of course, that's past tense now," She'd looked him in the eye as she asked him, "What is your problem, Sergeant Wilding? Why don't you believe me?"

Rob had felt sorry for her as he saw her eyes fill up with tears. He didn't like upsetting her and he had tried to explain his reasons. "It's not that I don't believe you, Miss Taylor. It's just that I have to be sure that I have covered everything. Look, I know it's hard and you don't understand why, but I really do have to ask these questions, however difficult and inappropriate they may seem to you. I'm just doing my job, its normal procedure."

He had seen the tension in her neck as she'd retaliated. "Well, this might be normal to you, but it most certainly is not normal 'procedure' to me. I'm not sure 'normal' will ever figure in my life again." Then she'd just sat there for a few moments in silence looking down at the floor before saying, in a much more controlled and quieter voice, "If you have finished with the questions, I would like you to leave now." And although he had left her house, he hadn't left the interview because several hours later he was still going over the conversation in his mind.

He was baffled because if it wasn't Sherry Taylor that Mrs Burrows had seen at 8.15 on that night, then who had it been?

He sighed, suddenly feeling exasperated.

With so many unresolved issues bouncing around inside his head he felt restless, so he dragged himself off the sofa, showered, and changed into something casual. He toyed with the idea of ringing Sophie but then decided against it and instead he sent his mate a text to see if he was out anywhere.

At the Swan, came his reply.

He picked up a warm coat and as he stepped out into the cold night air, he locked his front door behind him.

Rob walked briskly to the pub, which was a good twenty-five minutes away. It was a crisp frosty night, and he could see his own breath forming mini clouds of white in the night-air. He pulled his collar up around his neck and shoved his hands deep into his coat pockets. The full moon lit up the road ahead and even though it was cold, it was nice to be walking and breathing in the fresh crisp air. As he walked past his local, he could see clearly across to the other side of the road, where his boss was getting into a taxi with a woman. Rob hoped it was 'the woman' because that meant he would be in a good mood tomorrow.

"Fingers crossed," he said to himself.

Two games of darts later and Rob began to feel better, seeing his mate had lifted his mood. It had been long overdue. Well over a month had passed by since he had last seen him, so they put the world to rights over a few pints. Rob even managed to win one of the games of darts, which almost never happened.

As he walked home, he knew the weight of his work had lightened a little, and he felt pleased that he had made the effort.

CHAPTER TWENTY-ONE

"Jesus!" Strain gripped the headboard with both hands as an orgasm rumbled through his body. He pulled Christie down hard onto him and they lay there together, in silence, for a while.

Strain was lost in his own thoughts as he drifted off into a contented sleep. When he woke up, he stretched and turned over. He reached out his arm for Christie, but he was met by an empty space. Leaning up on one elbow he called out her name, thinking that maybe she was in the bathroom or in the kitchen, making a coffee for them both, but there came no reply. It looked like Christie had already left. He turned back to the empty space by his side and saw the note lying there on the pillow. He grabbed it and read it.

Once again a great night. See you soon, Christie. xx

As a wave of anger washed over him, he screwed it up into a tight ball and tossed it across the bedroom. "For Christ's sake" he said out loud. She had done it again; disappeared without leaving a contact number.

His night of passion was suddenly a distant memory. He slung back the duvet, got up and headed for the kitchen. After lighting a cigarette, he made a cup of coffee and sat on the stool. He couldn't work it out. Why the hell did she have this effect on him?

Sex-and-go had always been good enough in the past, so why do I want more from this one? What is so bloody special about her?

He stubbed out his cigarette, finished his coffee and slumped off to the bathroom to take a shower.

CHAPTER TWENTY-TWO

Rob was up and out to work early, feeling brighter than he had for a while. He was standing in the corridor chatting with Sophie, the cleaning lady. They regularly met up at the coffee machine. It was like their secret rendezvous place, and they were laughing and joking, and fooling around. They had been out on a couple of dates, but they were still in the early stages of getting to know each other and all he really knew was that she was the same age as him and she was single, which was enough to start with. He didn't like to ask too many questions too early on in a relationship because that was being a policeman and initially, he liked dating to be escapism. She had a great figure with a petite frame and shoulder-length black hair. Her eyes were deep brown in colour and had a gentle but reassuring look about them. He had seen her wearing glasses with thick lenses, but she always managed to push them up onto the top of her head whenever he got near to her so he figured that maybe she felt a bit self-conscious. He wondered if she might have a foreign connection in her bloodline because of the light Mediterranean colour of her skin.

They both turned and looked down the corridor as they heard a loud voice echo out through the office door:

"Bloody cow run dry this morning or what?"

"Great, not only is he early, but it sounds like he's in a right mood. I'd better get a move on." He got two coffees from the machine. "See you later," he said, as he left her and went into the office.

"You're early this morning, Guv, is everything okay?"

Strain was immediately on the defensive. "Why wouldn't it be?" He paused for a moment before saying. "Of course, everything would be a whole lot better if you were about to tell me you had solved at least one of our cases."

Rob pursed his lips tightly together and shook his head, but before he could say anything Strain was off again.

"Yeah well, why aren't I surprised. Call a team meeting. I want a progress update. And I think you need to pull that Taylor girl in for official questioning. I'm sure she's involved somehow." Strain sipped his steaming hot coffee, and fortunately, it seemed to have a calming effect on him.

"I agree," said Rob. "I don't know exactly where she fits in, but I reckon she's definitely a piece of the puzzle." He relayed the gist of the conversation he'd had with Sherry the day before. "How do you want to handle it? It's not like we can arrest her. We have nothing to charge her with. We need her to come in voluntarily, but to be honest, I feel confident when I say, that isn't going to happen. She all but told me to fuck off and leave her alone."

Strain was surprised that Rob agreed with him, he'd been adamant until now that she wasn't involved. He pinched at his chin and thought for a moment. "All right then, this is what we'll do. We'll put her under surveillance and watch her every move. Where she goes, what she does, who she sees. I'll leave that with you, okay?"

"Really," Rob sighed inwardly, feeling suddenly deflated. He hated surveillance work.

Strain ignored Rob's reaction and continued, "You know, I don't think it would do any harm if she was to see that you were watching her, it might unnerve her a little, maybe just enough to push her over the edge, and she might crack under pressure and make a mistake."

Rob nodded his agreement then sat down at his desk and typed out an email informing the rest of the team that an update meeting had been planned for later that day, he pressed send, then took the car keys off Strain and left the office.

Outside in the corridor he could see Sophie kneeling down, cleaning the bottom of a cupboard. She wasn't looking so he didn't speak as he walked past her and stepped into the lift that would take him down to the car park.

On his way over to Sherry Taylor's house, Rob stopped off at a shop. One of his pet hates was being stuck somewhere with no food or drink, so he bought supplies in the form of crisps and biscuits.

Very healthy.

Then, as if to compensate for choosing nothing but junk food, he grabbed a bottle of water, but then thinking he may need some caffeine, he added a couple of cans of coke and also a newspaper. Once he was satisfied that he had enough nibbles to keep him happy for the day, he set off.

He arrived at Taylor's house at 9.45 a.m. and parked up on the opposite side of the road. He shuffled in his seat and adjusted it to a more relaxed position and picked up the newspaper but he only managed to get as far as page four, when he saw her step out of her front door. She was looking straight at him as she crossed the road and walked towards his car.

Here we go.

He opened the window and smiled at her. It was clear to him that she was angry, but even so, standing there with her long blonde hair loose and shining in the winter morning sun, she looked lovely and it was hard for him to imagine her being involved in anything sinister. She stopped at the side of his car with her arms folded and she held his gaze as she spoke. "Can I help you with something, Sergeant Wilding?"

"No thanks, Miss Taylor," said Rob politely.

"This has to be some kind of harassment! I'm not a criminal and I don't deserve to be treated like one. You should know that I'm not going to put up with this," and with that she turned and marched back across the road and disappeared inside her house.

She re-emerged five minutes later with her coat on and carrying a bag, she got into her car and drove off.

Even though it was obvious that she knew he was there, Rob did as he had been instructed and kept to within two cars behind her all day long.

He was tired and irritable when he arrived back at the station. He chucked the car keys down onto Strain's desk. "Sixty-seven miles she's done today. She's led me a right merry dance. What does she think she is going to gain by behaving in this way?"

"She thinks she's going to get one over on us. Go home now, Rob. You can go back there in the morning. I'll sit outside her house tonight," he said as he picked up the car keys. "See how clever she thinks she is then. I'll show her we don't give up that easily!"

Relieved that Strain was going to cover the night watch, he said, "I missed the meeting. Are there any new developments that I should know about?"

"No. Nothing really. We still don't have any leads. I'll fill you in tomorrow. Come to the office before you go over to Taylors house and I'll catch you up on events."

Rob nodded, gathered some things up off his desk and left before his boss could change his mind.

Strain sat back in his chair and thought about the phone call he had received earlier from Chief Superintendent Ridley, informing him of the complaint he had received from a Miss Sherry Taylor regarding possible police harassment. Strain decided to ignore the warning as he finished up in the office and drove over to Taylor's house.

Unlike Rob, he hadn't bothered to bring anything with him to eat or drink. He parked up and adjusted the car seat until he was comfortable then he leaned his head back and closed his eyes.

What seemed like a few seconds later, he was startled by somebody knocking on the car window.

Shit, I must have dozed off.

He rubbed his eyes and sat up in his seat. He was surprised to see Christie standing there, and he almost jumped out of the car.

"Hi there," he said, running his hands through his hair.

"Hello Detective," she replied in a sultry voice. "What are you doing in my neighbourhood? Have you come to arrest me and put me in handcuffs?"

Her teasing was almost too much to bear: "I wish I had, but unfortunately, I'm on duty."

"Well, what time do you get off duty, Detective?"

Trying hard to disguise his lust for her, he looked at his watch. He couldn't believe it was 1 a.m. He must have been asleep for hours! He felt cross with himself for his botched surveillance job.

Trying not to show how he felt, he said, "I guess I could finish now," his eyes met hers, "Do you want to come with me?"

"I thought you'd never ask," she replied, and she held his gaze as she walked around his car and sat in the passenger seat. Strain looked over at Sherry Taylor's house. Her car was still parked in the same space, so hopefully he hadn't missed any activity. He got back into the driver's seat, and as he clipped his seat belt in place, Christie leaned in and kissed him, long and slow. Her tongue skilfully found his and played havoc with his senses.

As she pulled away, Strain took in a deep breath and said: "Best we get going then."

During the drive home, he struggled to concentrate. Her long legs were on display, and he found it hard to keep his eyes off them and on the road.

Thirty-five minutes later he opened the door to his apartment, and they barely made it inside before their lips found each other's, their tongues collided with a frenzied passion.

They had removed each other's clothes long before they reached his bed.

"Christie," he breathed.

"Shush," she whispered.

"But where have you been" he asked.

"Shush," she said again as she put her finger over his lips. "No talking." And with her tongue, she gently worked her way down from his lips to his groin.

CHAPTER TWENTY-THREE

Sherry was lying in bed trying, without success to fall asleep. She was restless, relentlessly shifting and turning over in a bid to get comfortable. She looked at the clock for what seemed like the hundredth time in as many seconds. She was tired, but she was wide awake.
It's that bloody copper's fault, he's the reason my mind is racing. How dare they watch me. Who do they think they are? Who do they think I am?
She was pleased with herself that she had managed to run Sergeant Wilding around on a wild goose chase this morning. Served him right, pretending to be the nice guy then pulling a stunt like that. She had spotted the same car parked outside again this evening, but she hadn't got the energy to do the same to whoever was inside it. Thankfully when she had checked half an hour or so earlier, she was relieved to find that it had gone. Still, the damage had been done, and try as she might she was finding it hard to settle her overactive mind. It was racing, filled to the brim with questions. After what seemed like an eternity, finally she began to relax but just as she was drifting off to sleep something made her jump. With eyes wide open she sat up in bed and let out a small squeal.

The light on the landing spilled through into her bedroom and was enough for her to see that it was Tracy.

"For god's sake, you startled me again." Sherry said irritably, as she reached over and switched on the lamp, "How many times do I have to ask you not to let yourself in whenever you feel like it? I imagine normal friends call or text before they visit, I'm not sure why it is so difficult for you to do that."

"Well," Tracy said with a mischievous look on her face, "you should know me by now. I like the element of surprise," and then she pouted as she feigned remorse. "I'm sorry, I know I'm a nightmare, but I had missed some calls from you this week, so I thought I'd pop in and surprise you and check that you're doing okay." Sherry noticed her friends face cloud over as she added. "And also, because I needed to warn you."

"Warn me?" Sherry asked, unable to hide her surprise at this statement. "What do you mean 'warn me'? What about?"

"They are on to you," Tracy said in a serious voice, and as she studied her friend, she added; "but you already know that don't you?"

"What are you talking about? Who's on to me?" Sherry asked in a mystified tone. "I haven't done anything wrong!"

"Oh, but you have, Sherry. Don't you remember? Think hard. Think really hard, my beautiful friend."

Sherry tried to keep down the panic that had lurched into her throat, but it was leaking a vile taste into her mouth. This woman who was standing in front of her was her life-long friend, and yet suddenly she felt afraid of her.

Why was she behaving like this?

Sherry swallowed hard. "You're not making any sense, Tracy. Shall we go downstairs? I could make us a drink and you can explain to me what you mean and what it is that you think I've done."

Tracy nodded. "Yes, good idea. Let's Do that."

CHAPTER TWENTY-FOUR

The next morning Rob walked into the office and was surprised to find Strain sitting at his desk. "Morning Guv."

"Alright, Rob," Strain looked up briefly, but he didn't maintain any eye contact and he quickly looked down again.

"How'd it go last night?" Rob asked.

"What do you mean?" Strain shouted a little louder than he needed to.

Rob furrowed his brow. "Sherry Taylor, did she go anywhere or do anything?"

"Oh, er, no. Not a dickey bird from her!" He felt his cheeks colour slightly.

Rob turned to face Strain and with genuine concern asked, "Is everything all right, Guv?"

Strain didn't take kindly to being pushed. "No, I'm not okay. There's a bloody murderer out there on the loose and we are no further forward now than we were two months ago." He picked up his mug and stormed out of the office, leaving a bewildered young assistant sitting there.

Strain had known from a very young age that he was going to pursue a career in the police force. His Grandfather had been a detective and he had vivid memories of sitting on the floor, listening wide-eyed to Gramps' stories. He had made it all sound exciting, and Strain could hardly wait to grow up and become a detective himself. He had worked hard at school and then gone on to attend further education at String Mill

College, where he'd taken a degree. In order to become a police officer, he'd had to pass several written exams, but it wasn't all about being academic, Police officers need to be fast on their feet, so being agile and in good shape were also important factors. He had sailed through his two-year probationary period and had worked his way up the career ladder one rung at a time to eventually achieve his goal. Which is why he was cross with himself now; even his wife, Maggie, had known she was going to come in second place, and his job was always going to come first. This was, of course, the main reason that she was now his ex-wife.

They had met when they were just sixteen and had dated on and off for a couple of years, but Strain had needed to put his studies first and concentrate on getting the grades required to achieve his chosen career, so he had ended their relationship. Then quite by accident a few years later, he had bumped into her at a bar in their hometown. Neither one of them had planned to be there that night, both had been dragged along by well-meaning friends, so believing that fate had played a hand in their reunion, they had picked up exactly where they'd left off. He was still in love with her, and it wasn't long before he'd proposed and they were married. Life was good for the next five years but then the pressure had started. Maggie had always wanted children, so when she announced that she was ready to start a family and bring some normality into their lives, although he wasn't surprised, these were things that Strain was not able to give her at the time and their fairy-tale had ended badly in divorce. As a result of this he was left devastated and disillusioned with life, and he had gone on to become a playboy, with serious commitment issues.

He had continued to bounce around between short relationships and one night stands ever since.

This was genuinely the first time he had ever let a woman distract him from his job and he was surprised at the situation he found himself in, it's like she had taken over his mind and his body. Christie left him sexually satisfied but mentally frustrated.

CHAPTER TWENTY-FIVE

I dragged the lifeless corpse into the bushes and as I straightened up, I looked around to make sure there wasn't an audience lurking anywhere. I took the chiffon scarf from my pocket and folded it into a neat triangle before placing it over her eyes. There wasn't much of anything on the ground that was suitable to hide her with so I covered up her body as best I could, with a thin layer of the crispy brown bracken which was scattered about in small piles and then I stood there for a moment reflecting. Once again, I had achieved the perfection that I always strived to reach. It had gone exactly to plan!

I saw her.
I strangled her.
I watched her die.

It was magnificent, so fulfilling! Revenge is such a wonderful thing. I'd felt like I wanted to sing out loud as I'd witnessed the life drain from her eyes. That, and the added bonus of her final strangulated plea: "Please don't hurt me, I have a baby daughter. She needs me. I'll do anything you want."

What a hit, a double whammy. Serves her right, greedy bitch, thinking that she can have a career and a family.

Lately things hadn't been going too well, what with distractions and do-gooders, but in the end it always comes to those who wait. It made me smile as I recalled the phrase my old Gran used to say, and it had – come to me - and it was perfectly done. I was so busy flattering myself that I hadn't noticed the dog who was sniffing around behind me. Its tail was wagging as it made a beeline for my buried treasure.

Suddenly, in the distance, I heard a female voice call out, "Tillie? Come here girl."

Startled by the voice and without looking, I pulled up my hood and I ran. Luckily, the dog was more interested in what it had found than it was in chasing after me. It was less than two minutes later when I heard the loud screams of the woman. Her shrill tones filled the air as they echoed through the parkland, but I just kept running and didn't stop until I reached my car. I didn't even have time to catch my breath, I was inside it like a flash and I started the engine and as I drove off the adrenalin was pumping around my body like a herd of wild horses galloping through my veins, making me feel light-headed.

I took the back roads to avoid any cameras catching me leaving the area at the time my victim had been discovered and fifty-five minutes later, with my heart still pounding, I turned the key in my front door and went straight into the kitchen. I made a hot drink, took it into the lounge and put the telly on. Still brimming over with excitement, I sat on the sofa, drinking my coffee, waiting eagerly for the news update. I became increasingly impatient as I listened to the young presenter droning on about the weather forecast for the local area and then there was the national weather forecast, it seemed to be taking forever.

"Oh come on," I said to the television screen. "Nobody is interested in the bloody weather forecast, get on with the important stuff." And then - there it was – the breaking news. My early morning jog had already made the headlines. I sat there feeling proud as my conquest was reported.

"Good morning, this is Holly Jones, keeping you up to date with the latest headlines as and when we get them. Our top story this morning is the discovery of yet another woman's body. This time, in Hartley Woods. This is the third murdered woman to be found within the last three months. I'm sure that the question on most peoples' lips this morning is: Do we have a serial killer on the loose? The victim who has not yet been named was found by a woman out walking her dog at 7.00, this morning. Apparently, a nurse by trade, she checked for a pulse and was able to establish that the woman was indeed dead, but the victim's body was still warm, and raising fears that the killer might still be somewhere close by she ran back to her car and locked herself inside it before calling the police. An unconfirmed report states that the body was discovered in similar circumstances to the previous victims, barely covered over with only a thin layer of bracken. This raises a number of questions for me, which I'm sure you will all agree need to be answered. For instance: Was the killer disturbed or was it an intentional half-hearted attempt to hide them. Did the murderer want or maybe even need these bodies to be found? Stay with us as we talk to a top psychiatrist, who tries to explain how the mind of a murderer works and how their actions can be attributed to something that may have happened to them during their childhood. We'll be back right after this short break. Once again this has been Holly Jones for network TV, your trusted news provider."

"No, no, no. What the....? Shut the fuck up!" I screamed at my television "What the hell do you know about my childhood? Fuck-all actually, Miss Know-it-all."

I got to my feet. "I'm going to get you for saying that you fucking bitch!"

I was shaking from head to toe as I paced angrily up and down. I tried to think straight and come up with a plan to right this wrong that she had done. Satisfied with my decision, I went back outside, slamming the front door behind me. I got into my car, started the engine, and reversed off my drive so fast that I almost ran over my neighbour's cat.

'Stupid fucking animal," I cursed. "I'll get you next time."

I drove my car towards Shipley Park, which, although was only a forty-minute drive in the opposite direction to Hartley Woods, the early morning traffic was heavy, and it seemed to take me forever to get there. This only served to fuel my anger and I found myself shaking with fury as I took the slip road off the dual carriageway and U-turned under the bridge towards the park.

The veins in my neck felt dangerously close to exploding as I arrived and abandoned my car haphazardly in the car park. As I pulled a pair of leather gloves out of my pocket and put them on, I pulled my hood up and made my way up one of the tracks that would lead me into the woodland. I stopped and looked around, but there was no one about. Feeling disappointed, I turned around to try a different pathway and then I saw her - one very unlucky solo jogger.

Breathing heavily, I walked straight up to her, and I could see that she had more of an indignant look on her face rather than one of fear. Clearly, she didn't realise what was about to happen and she had no time to react as I punched her straight in the face and she hit the ground. She landed hard, and I kicked her in the stomach. I kept on kicking at her head and her stomach, until she fell silent.

In broad daylight I had killed her, without giving a single thought to who else might be around. It was over so quickly that she didn't even have a chance to object to her looming fate.

I left her broken lifeless body where it had fallen, with a bright coloured chiffon scarf covering her eyes.

There, now put me in a category, news reader bitch! See how clever you think you are now. This one was your fault. Live with that, Miss Holly Jones!

Out of breath and still in a rage, I ran back to my car and discarded my gloves in a bag in the boot, then I drove home. This time though, I took my boots off on the doorstep, carried them inside and deposited them into a bin bag, then I went straight upstairs and into the bathroom. I stripped off my soiled clothing and put them into an old laundry bag, I would burn them later on this evening.

My mind was in turmoil as I got in the shower, but the combination of the hot water and the sweet-smelling gel was soothing and persuasive in calming me down.

Feeling in a lighter mood I got dressed and after deciding to skip breakfast, I left for work.

CHAPTER TWENTY-SIX

"Two within hours of each other, Guv. What the hell happened?"

"I don't know, Rob, I've never known this to happen before."

"I think I might know," a female voice interrupted them.

Rob and Strain both turned around at the same time to see an attractive woman with short black hair standing in the office doorway.

Strain raised his eyebrows and said: "And who might you be?"

"I'm Sandy Moore, from the behavioural squad, or more accurately, the resident forensic psychologist." She said as she walked towards them. "For future reference, my department is on the fourth floor and our job is to study, in depth, the minds of psychopaths and such like. Then hopefully, we can offer forward, important information in the form of a profile of your murderer."

Chief Superintendent Ridley had asked Rob to share the case notes on the murders with this specialist team. Apparently, he had previously told Strain to deal with them, but not surprisingly that hadn't happened. Rob remembered taking the lift up to their office and handing the file to a young geeky-looking guy. Sandy Moore was a huge improvement.

Without invite she continued with her opening speech. "In my opinion, I think that your killer was watching or listening to the news this morning when the first murder was being reported. I'm not saying that it was the news reader's fault by any means, but the way in which Holly Jones worded her report ridiculed the killer and the news line she chose to go with drove him into an uncontrollable frenzy which led him to make the decision to go straight out and kill again. Although the M.O. was not exactly the same as the previous murders, she was a jogger, and when I spoke to the pathologist earlier on, he did say that he thought her injuries had been dealt through rage."

Strain looked directly at her as he said, "You've already been to our crime scene?"

"No, I called him on his mobile," she said in a firm voice and then carried on speaking. "Now correct me if I'm wrong, but I believe one of your previous victims was beaten to death. This signifies that the murderer runs on a short fuse and there is no justification, rhyme, or reason behind these murders. He's just killing them because he can or because he wants to, more than likely out of an act of revenge. Unfortunately for us, this makes my job, as a profiler, much more difficult because revenge killings are very personal and if you can't find a connection between your victims and you don't know what the motive is for their murders, then there is a lot of guesswork involved. I personally think you should have a word with the press office, in particular, Holly Jones, and warn them to be more careful in future on how they report these murders. If they insult him further, you might just find he will go off on a wild killing spree."

"Oh, okay, I get it," Strain nodded knowingly. "So, what we've got here is quite a sensitive murderer then. Would you believe it, he's got feelings? Let's be careful how we talk about him because we wouldn't want to offend him, now, would we?" He turned away shaking his head.

Rob chipped in quickly in an attempt to calm his boss's temper. "I understand what you mean, Miss Moore. I saw the news report this morning and now that you've pointed it out, yes, I think you're right, she did insult him. It definitely came across in such a way that could have made the murderer angry, like he was an amateur and only doing it because of a crappy childhood. She judged him and put a label on him. I think I can see how that might have pissed him off."

"Unbelievable," Strain said, as he stomped out of the office.

Sandy watched as Strain disappeared from sight and said, "I see your killer is not the only one around here who is sensitive!"

"Ignore him," Rob said. "He doesn't mean anything by it. He's just frustrated with our lack of progress. So, what else can you tell us about our guy?"

"Not a great deal yet, but I'm working on it. I'll let you know as soon as I come up with a profile." She turned to leave and then stopped. She looked back at Rob and said, "Although, I can tell you this much: Don't be surprised to find out that your killer might be a woman. In fact, it's much more likely, because the victims after being killed had their face covered with a chiffon scarf. I consider this to be a feminine touch, so I'm not convinced that your murderer is a man."

Rob raised his eyebrows, "Whoa! Really? You tend to make the assumption that the killer is a bloke, but a woman… That's a new one on me."

At that moment Strain came back into the room with two coffees, one for Rob and one for himself. As he put the coffee cups down on the desk he looked over to Rob: "What's a new one on you?"

"She, Miss Moore, says our killer could well be a woman."

"That's an interesting theory. Have you got anything else to add, Miss Moore, or just that our killer is female and sensitive?"

"She's likely sociopathic too,"

Strain continued with his mocking by repeating what he had already said. "So just to be clear and to make sure that I fully understand, you are saying that our murderer is," and he made the sign with his fingers to show inverted commas as he said, "possibly female, sensitive and oh yes, has sociopathic tendencies!"

"Your reputation precedes you DCI Strain" she said and slammed the office door behind her as she left.

"That was unnecessary ridicule, Guv, you shouldn't be so hard on her. There's quite a lot to this profiling."

"Really, Rob, I expected more from you."

Rob went to fetch himself a fresh cup of coffee because the one Strain had given him was overloaded with sugar and he didn't take sugar. As he turned the corner, he could see Sophie was there wiping down the drinks machine:

She saw him coming, and as he got close enough, she said, in a lowered voice, "Sounds like he's got a right one on him this morning,"

Rob sighed, "tell me about it. I think the poor woman from upstairs, has just realised that she may have her work cut out and that our DCI hasn't yet evolved into the bright new world of modern technology, but is somehow trapped in a time warp of traditional policing."

They both laughed.

He got his coffee and said, "I had better get going. I wouldn't want to miss any fun moments in the life and times of DCI Strain." He smiled at her and then as he turned to go back to the office he stopped and said, "Do you fancy meeting for a drink later?"

"She blushed and nodded. "Yes, that would be really nice."

Trying not to look too surprised that she was willing to go out on a third date with him, he said, "Great, shall I meet you at the Cricketers Arms at around 8.00, then?"

She nodded her agreement and said, "See you later."

CHAPTER TWENTY-SEVEN

Crime Scene Investigators were all over the place by the time Strain and Rob got to the most recent murder scene. They both took plastic gloves from their pockets and a young officer handed them each a face mask and shoe covers. Then they made their way over to the tent that had been erected to protect the body and the crime scene from further contamination. As they entered the tent the pathologist greeted them with a grim face as he confirmed that it had been a frenzied attack, similar to the murder that had taken place in Shut Field a few months earlier where Jenna Hopkins had been beaten to death in what had also seemed like an anger attack. He ended his account with, "This murderer of yours is totally unhinged and spiralling out of control."

Strain ignored the pathologists last comment and asked, "Do you think they were both killed by the same person?"

"I can't be certain," he replied. "I'll know more once I get her back to my lab, but if I was to hazard a guess, then I would lean towards a yes."

"Right." Strain stood there looking down at the dead body of the young woman. Her face was covered with black, blue, and purple-coloured bruises and it was swollen to at least twice its normal size. There were thick clots of dried blood entwined in her hair.

He turned his head away, sickened by the sight of this poor woman's injuries, whose only mistake this morning was to have been in the wrong place at the wrong time.

"I don't think the word 'anger' quite covers it," he said quietly, as he started to walk away. "Let me know your findings as soon as you can."

The pathologist nodded his reply, and Strain and Rob left the crime scene to begin their journey in the opposite direction to the one that had taken place first. They travelled in silence. engrossed in their own thoughts.

Rob was the first to speak. "I wonder why he picks on joggers and why only women? Why at all? What's wrong with this person that makes him or her want to kill? It's not sexually motivated, and why does he seem to choose strangulation as his method, but then occasionally he changes tact and chooses to beat someone to death."

"I don't know, Rob, maybe he's not strong enough to take on men." He let out a sigh and shook his head. "He most probably uses strangulation because it's slow and painful. It could be that he gets a kick out of watching them die slowly or that he likes to look at their faces or maybe he makes them beg for their lives. Who knows what goes through his mind? He's just an evil bastard. Maybe the people he strangles are the real target and the ones that were beaten to death are a random kill, unplanned but necessary to satisfy his needs. Or just maybe, Miss Profiler from the fourth floor is right, and the news report did spark off some cranky reaction in him."

"Or her," Rob added thinking back to what Sandy Moore had said earlier.

Strain thought about what Rob had just said.

Why the hell can't we catch this monster? How is he managing to evade us?

The lack of CCTV coverage around parks and woodland didn't help, but maybe the murderer knew this and that was the reason why he chose to target these particular areas.

Strain already had his people studying the road network CCTV in and around the estimated time zones of all the murders, but it was an arduous and slow task, and he wasn't expecting any results anytime soon.

His thoughts switched to the previous night and for the first time he found himself wondering about Christie, and what she might have been doing in that particular area on the night of his stake-out. He didn't believe in coincidence, and if she lived in the neighbourhood, then surely she would have invited him back to her place, instead of driving over half an hour away to his flat. He thought about her uncanny resemblance to Sherry Taylor and even though he had only seen Taylor once for a matter of seconds, it had been long enough to flag an alarm and raise his suspicions.

What if she had been lying? What if she knew her or was related to her or worse still – was her?

He broke his train of thought and glanced sideways at Rob. "Are you okay? That was a tough scene to attend, even for me."

"Not really. To be honest it has shaken me up. I mean to think that a person is capable of delivering such horrendous fatal injuries to another human being. I honestly don't know how you have done this job for so long. I'm not sure I will be able to."

"Unfortunately, it's a horrible fact that you do harden up. I'm not saying that you ever get used to seeing violent and distressing scenes, but somehow you find a way of detaching yourself from them. Having a good social life helps. Have you got one Rob, a social life?"

"Yes, and I'm meant to be going out on a date tonight, but I'm thinking that I probably shouldn't go. I don't think I will be very good company; this case is eating away at me."

"Anyone I might know?" Strain asked, discreetly trying to clarify a rumour he had heard.

"Actually, yes, Sophie. She works here at the station; we've been out on a couple of dates already. She seems really nice."

Strain smiled to himself as Rob, confirmed the rumour to be true and then went on to say: "Don't cancel your date. You need to keep a solid link with the real world. When you finish work you have to be able to shut all the shit of the day in a cupboard and go and enjoy yourself. That cupboard will be right where you left it, waiting for you to open it again the next morning."

Rob was not convinced as he nodded his reply and parked the car outside the station, where there were hordes of journalists at the front doors, all hungry for a story.

"Here we go" Strain said. "What the hell do I tell them?"

"I'm sure you will think of something, Guv" Rob said lightly, trying to be helpful.

But it backfired.

"Oh, you're sure that I will think of something. Really, just what do you think this is all about Rob? Whether I drink tea or coffee. Whatever I tell them goes straight to the public, and you'd do well to remember that. So if we don't know anything for certain, then we don't tell them bloody vampires jack shit!"

"I didn't mean it like that, Guv. I just meant that you think quick and..."

But Strain didn't wait to hear anymore. As he got out of the car, he slammed the door shut, and pushed his way through the eager reporters. He kept his head down, ignoring the barrage of questions they were shouting at him.

"Is it a serial killer?"

"Have you got any leads yet?"

"Don't you think you have a duty to inform the public?"

"Come on DCI Strain, talk to us."

As he pushed through the double doors which led inside the station, he felt a sudden pang of guilt for the verbal attack he had just launched at Rob, but that soon passed, and he stopped at the coffee machine before heading to their office.

CHAPTER TWENTY-EIGHT

Sherry Taylor could not believe her eyes when she put on the TV and saw that there had been two more murders that morning, the second one, within hours of the first one. She shuddered at the thought that someone could be so out of control and on the loose.

She was sitting in her pyjamas drinking a cup of tea, and, as she put her mug down, she reached over to the coffee table and picked up one of the many kitchen brochures that she had collected the day before and began looking at the pages she had turned the corner edge over on. Although she had received it under tragic circumstances, her inheritance had indeed changed her life. Mrs Johnson had left her very well-off, and after much soul searching, she had decided to leave her job and concentrate on giving her own house a much-needed makeover.

She had lived in it for almost three years and during that time, she hadn't really done much to improve it, but now with a decent budget in her bank, she had it all planned out. The first thing on her list was to have a new fitted kitchen, complete with appliances, followed by a new bathroom, with a free-standing shower cubicle rather than having to climb into the bath to take a shower. The remaining rooms just needed some fresh decoration and new carpets, although she was considering having wooden flooring fitted throughout the downstairs. She had already contacted a company that supplied and fitted double-glazing units and they were due out next week to give her a quote. She had been delighted when they told her they were currently running an offer whereby you paid for the front windows of the house and got the back windows free. These tasks were all about keeping her occupied and giving her something positive to focus on whilst she adapted to her new life. She was still waiting to hear from, Mr Sharman, the solicitor, who was dealing with Mrs Johnson's estate. He said he would be in touch as soon as the police released Mrs Johnson's house, but it could be several months yet as it was still part of a live investigation and therefore an active crime scene. She had decided that once it was turned over to her, she was going to sell it, even though it was a lovely old house and quite a lot bigger than her own, she had no desire to live there, as it would be a constant reminder of the terrible fate that had prematurely ended the life of her friend. It had been well-maintained over the years and was in good repair, but even so, it needed a bit of updating and a lick of paint before marketing. There was certainly enough to keep her busy for at least the next year, and for that she was grateful.

Sherry picked up her cup and finished the contents and then sat back in her chair.

Three years! How time had flown.

She would have liked to have met a man by now and perhaps fallen in love. She had thought that by moving to a new area, different opportunities would have opened up for her but her life, so far, had been a quiet one. Even her crazy friend, Tracy, appeared to have abandoned her, for whatever reason, which made her sad, because although she was a total pain in the ass, she missed her terribly. Sherry decided that she would give her a ring later and arrange a night out together. It would do her good to get out and let her hair down, they could go to a night club. Although Sherry was under no illusion, she knew Tracy already had an active social life that she wasn't a part of. Nevertheless, Sherry's spirits were lifted at the mere thought of having fun. It would be a good thing when she could put the recent tragic events behind her and begin to enjoy her life again. And because she'd been able to pay off her own mortgage in full, with the cash that Mrs Johnson had left her, she knew life could be good for her again.

She had made an effort and been to see Mrs Alderson and said goodbye to her, there was no love lost as she had never been close to this woman, it was just sad to leave her old life behind because it had been a happy one. That said, she knew in time, she would begin to enjoy her new one, she also knew that would happen a lot quicker if the police would stay off her back. They had been watching her every move lately and she found their actions to be very upsetting and it left her baffled with no idea why they thought she might somehow be involved in the death of Mrs Johnson.

She got up and walked over to the front window, lifted the blind and saw that they weren't outside today. Maybe the call she had made to a, Chief Superintendent Ridley, threatening to sue them for harassment, had worked. She hoped so. She also hoped that they were doing a more important job; like trying to find the real nut job that was out there killing women.

CHAPTER TWENTY-NINE

Rob arrived back at the office feeling sheepish after Strain's outburst regarding the journalists fronting the building. He updated the incident board with the names of the latest victims. The first victim was Miss Tina Scott, aged twenty-five and a single mom. She was the one who had been strangled. And the second victim was Barbara Wayne, aged twenty-nine and married. She was the one who had been brutally beaten to death. This brought the total number of murder victims to four. He moved to sit at his desk and set about the task of re-reading the files on all the victims to date, in the hope of finding something that may have previously been missed, something that might just link them together.

In the meantime, Strain put a call in to Holly Jones, the news reader. He dialled the number on her website, courtesy of Rob. He thought he should have a quiet word with her regarding the way in which she had delivered her report earlier, but the call diverted straight to her voicemail, so he left a brief message asking her to call him back as soon as she could. He followed that with a direct call to the Network office, again she was unavailable, but the receptionist said she would pass his message on. He replaced the receiver and looked over at Rob: "I've been meaning to ask; did you check out the chiffon scarves?"

"Yes I did and although they are a very popular item with hundreds being sold through a variety of outlets across the

UK, not one of these outlets has a record of ever selling an extraordinarily high amount to any one person, and although we can't rule out bankrupt stock being sold through an auction house, it's hard to track because they are usually sold in lots. There is a department store in Bournemouth that stocks them, and I had someone call in to see them, but it's such a small item and again, although they are popular, they don't keep a record of whose buying them. So, there are no leads there to follow."

Their conversation was disturbed by the sound of the phone on Strain's desk ringing. He picked it up. "Yeah, Strain here, really. Okay. Let me know if it turns out to be anything useful." He replaced the handset and turned to face Rob. "Good news. Some material has been found, caught on a branch, at the first of the two crime scenes. Hopefully, it belongs to our killer's clothes. It's not great but it's a start."

Rob looked impressed. "Thank goodness, a breakthrough at last."

"We can but hope. If it's not a piece of the victim's clothing, then we'll assume it's our killer's. With any luck, they might get some DNA from it and if it matches to a person who is already logged on the national database, then we can bring them in for questioning. If they haven't got an alibi for the times of the murders, then we will have a lead."

Rob nodded his head. He had always known that murder investigations were a lot more scientific than the operations of the fraud squad, but he had been quite blinkered to the workings of any other departments outside of his own. It was only now that he realised how tedious it actually was to find the smallest clue and work with it.

Strain continued. "Once we have the results, if it warrants it, I want you to bring Miss Taylor in. There is something about that woman that bugs me, so we'll get a sample of her DNA, if only to eliminate her from our enquiries once and for all. I don't think for one minute that she is our serial killer, but I do enjoy pissing her off!" Strain could see Rob's face drop.

"Great, that's something to look forward to. "I don't think she'll come in voluntarily."

"Don't worry about that now, we'll get a court order if necessary, and to be honest if she's not involved, then it shouldn't bother her. Trust me. she'll be glad to get us off her back." Strain said, confidently.

"I don't think it's personal," Rob, said. "She only dislikes us because her life has been upset and she needs someone to yell at."

"Well, whatever her reasons are for disliking us, we still need to process her just the same as we would anyone else whose name continually keeps cropping up in our enquiries."

CHAPTER THIRTY

As far as I can remember, until today, there hasn't been a time when I didn't enjoy my work. All day, I had tried, somewhat unsuccessfully, to forget the reporter's comments from this morning's news desk regarding the headline - my headline - but her words had churned over and over, almost burning themselves into my mind. So, with my working day finally finished, I headed home with the full intention of relaxing, but deep feelings of restlessness were leaving me feeling irritable and unsettled. Holly Jones's words had been echoing through my head all day, and still were. They were playing on my mind, like an old record with the needle stuck, and my bad mood hadn't gone unnoticed by my work colleagues because they had given me a wide berth for most of my shift, and even now, several hours later, I was still feeling hateful and wound up inside. Damn that news reporter, the day had started off so well, and then she'd spoilt everything.

I had felt triumphant with my first kill of the day. It had been perfectly planned and perfectly executed. The second victim though was unnecessary; she shouldn't have been killed, I mean I'm not a monster, except for the odd hic-cup, there are legitimate and genuine reasons for my killings.

I sat down with a hot drink, quietly mulling over my thoughts and trying to process the day's events in my mind but the feelings of anger that I hadn't managed to suppress, once again began to rise to the surface, bubbling away like a hot pot turned up too high on the gas. That stupid cow had judged me; she thought she knew all about me and she had even been confident enough to share her so-called knowledge with the rest of the world on live TV, making me out to be some sort of insecure failure that has been scarred by a crappy upbringing. What a bitch! Well, she's wrong. I don't do this to get attention. I do it purely for my own satisfaction. For revenge. Not as a cry for help to society or to make amends for a fucked-up childhood. What she does as a TV news presenter, that's for attention; so that when she goes out in public, people recognise her. Yes, she's talking about herself. Well, she'll be sorry she ever voiced an opinion about me. She'll get the fame she so obviously craves when she's the headlines – when she's the so-called breaking news.

   I had been pacing up and down for quite a while, I was worked up, and I felt hot and sweaty as I went upstairs and got into the shower. I lavished in the lather, gently smoothing it all over my body, engulfing myself in the potent smell of freesia that filled my nostrils. It made me think of summer and sunshine and I felt uplifted as I dried myself and slipped on my towelling robe. I pulled the chord tight and went back downstairs feeling a lot better. I made a cup of coffee and sat down at my computer. As soon as I touched the mouse the screen sprang into life, and I began my research. I typed the name 'Holly Jones' into Google search and smiled at the many listings that appeared on the screen.

   Right then, Miss Jones, let's see if we can find out where you live.

CHAPTER THIRTY-ONE

The Forensics team had finished processing the piece of fabric that had been discovered at the first of the most recent crime scenes and they were able to confirm that it was not part of the victim's clothing, although at one stage there was still a chance that it could have been torn from the murderer's clothing instead, but a more detailed test revealed there was no DNA present, which can be the case, particularly if it was part of an over-garment. So, with no DNA there was nothing to check it against. Strain listened intently to what Ed, from the lab, was saying to him and he couldn't help feeling deflated by the outcome. He had pinned his hopes on this being their first breakthrough. He finished on the phone and turned to face Rob. "Bad news, there's no DNA present on the snagged fabric to run through the data base."

Rob's shoulders sagged as he sighed and said: "Back to square one then. So what do we do next? How are we supposed to catch this person when we have absolutely nothing to work with?"

Strain instantly stepped up to reassure him, showcasing the years of experience he had. "Don't sound so defeated. This person might be a mystery to us at the moment, but trust me, all it will take is one small thing to happen and although it might not seem significant at the time, suddenly the murky picture will begin to clear. This is why it is so important to keep reading the reports, and re-reading any statements to make absolutely certain that we haven't missed anything. As tedious as it may be, it's the only way."

Rob nodded and said, "What about Sandy Moore?"

Strains sympathetic attitude dissolved instantly. "What about her?"

"Well, do you think we should involve her? I, for one, think we should. I can't see what harm it will do, and you never know, she might even help us to see something we're missing."

Strain thought for a moment and then with a defeatist sigh, said: "Yeah, go on then, why not? What have we got to lose?"

CHAPTER THIRTY-TWO

Sandy Moore was thirty-one years old. She was single and content. Her social life was virtually non-existent because her dedication to her job made it difficult for her to commit to a full-time relationship, but in her eyes, doing the job she loved was worth more than a hundred dates, so she had decided there would be plenty of time in the future for men, once she had established her career. All her young life she had been interested in people. She had kept a private journal on human behaviour amongst her classmates, analysing them, and trying to understand what they did and why they did it. She had constantly tried to work out why some were bigheads, and some were bullies, obviously being careful not to mention any names. There was always a reason for their behaviour and Sandy had enjoyed secretly studying them in a bid to find out what lay behind their personalities.

Her journey through school and college and finally university, had resulted in her graduating with a degree in psychology and sociology. Her interest in human behaviour had never waned and now it was her job, and she was damn good at it.

Her email alert pinged and disturbed her thoughts. She smiled to herself as she opened an email from Sergeant Rob Wilding.

"Ha," she said out loud, as she read his invitation to assist them with their case. "Welcome to the twenty first century."

She closed the folder that she had been reading and locked it away in the filing cabinet. Picking up her brief case she checked that it contained the profile she had already written before taking the lift down to CID.

She'd foolishly thought that maybe because they had contacted her that both Strain and Rob would be on board, but the realisation struck her like a slap to her face as it instantly became clear that Rob was a lot more enthusiastic about profiling than his boss, Strain, was. But nevertheless, she hoped it wouldn't be long before she hooked him in too, and in her opinion, it was inevitable that he would eventually come to realise the importance of profiling. She knew her biggest hurdle would be getting Strain to listen, but once she had achieved that goal, she felt confident that she would be able to add valuable insight for them, which in turn would help them to understand how the murderer's mind worked and this alone was priceless.

"Good morning," Sandy said in an upbeat tone.

"Hi there, Miss Moore," Rob said.

"Sandy, please." She smiled at him.

Rob smiled back and nodded.

"Are you always this cheerful in the morning?" Strain asked.

"Yes, I am. Should I be apologising for that?" Sandy replied, undeterred by his arrogant look as she continued to speak. "Shall we get everyone who is working on the case to gather round so that we can work through this profile together?"

"I think I'd prefer it if we took option two," Strain said, looking her in the eyes. "How about you run your 'profile' by the two of us first, then we'll decide if it's informative enough to share with the rest of the team."

As the hairs on the back of her neck prickled, Sandy fought back the urge to tell Strain he was an immature prick and instead she replied with, "Sure thing. Whatever you say." She even managed to force a smile.

Strain sat back in his chair with a smirk on his face and his feet on the desk and said, "Over to you then, Miss Moore."

Sandy cleared her throat and bit on her lower lip as she swallowed unnecessarily. She was cross with herself for allowing Strain to unnerve her. She took a file out of her brief case and she ran her finger along the edge, then she swiftly opened it, took in a deep breath, and lifted her head: "The first thing I would like to point out is that the death of Mrs Johnson, in my opinion, is in no way connected to the murders of these young women."

"Tell us something we don't already know," Strain said under his breath, but loud enough for Sandy to hear.

Rob cut him a sharp look, but Sandy blanked him out and managed to maintain a professional attitude as she continued. "Okay, the sort of person you are dealing with here has no natural boundaries. There is no 'off' switch in their brain alerting them to stop what they are doing. We all know the meaning of right and wrong, including sociopaths, but in general, they choose to ignore it." She briefly made eye contact with Rob as she carried on delivering her profile. "They have no emotional compulsion to conform and if there is even the slightest threat of a punishment this will only serve as a greater challenge to them. As a rule, they are natural risk-takers because they do not experience anxiety like most of us would, and although this person I am describing is a typical sociopath, they are not generally murderers. Not intentionally anyway. So, I am going to include the added bonus of psychopathic tendencies and we may also be able to add a touch of schizophrenia into the mix."

"Crikey, nice combination," said Rob.

"I think it's called, 'covering your options'," Strain scoffed.

Sandy glanced over at him again but continued to speak. "People with these conditions will have a total lack of remorse and shame and are completely irrational in their thinking. Now this doesn't necessarily mean that this person will be a down and out as they are award winners when it comes to deception and could quite easily be a successful and professional person. Physically speaking, I believe they will be high up in the fitness league, as they will more than likely work out every day. They will need to do this to enable them to have the strength and the stamina to take on their victims with ease and without any fuss. I have previously mentioned to you that I believe your killer to be a woman and I stand by this. As I read through your case notes, I think that a strong feminine presence is evident. At the moment though, I can't come up with a valid reason why she has chosen to target these women, as there is nothing apparent that links them together. I am, however, thinking it's a strong possibility that she herself jogs and that is how she targets her victims and also how she would be aware of the quiet times to strike. With the exception of her last attack, which was frenzied, uncalculated and unplanned. My guess is that she was driven to this by the words of the news reader, Holly Jones, whom she thought had insulted and belittled her."

Strain suddenly realised that he hadn't heard back from Holly Jones, and he made a mental note to call her again. He turned his attention back to Sandy Moore, who was still speaking.

"This then made her angry enough to put herself in a high-risk situation where she was not put off by the possible consequences of being caught, if anything, I imagine it may have excited her. Looking at her personal life, she more than likely won't be in a steady relationship as she will think love is exceedingly unreliable, so she probably just has casual sexual relations when she needs them and whether she likes to admit it or not, her behaviour, or condition, will have been brought on by events from her childhood. She will hate this label because she likes to be in full control of her life at all times." She paused for a moment as Strain removed his feet from the desk and she thought she'd lost him.

"You've just described most of the women I've ever met." He said.

Rob was far more positive: "That's really good and well-thought-out. It makes a lot of sense to me."

Sandy felt her shoulders relax slightly as she concluded. "So, in my opinion, you are looking for a female. Her age group will more than likely be in or around thirty years old, possibly a professional and living a life that outwardly appears to be normal, and maybe even fun-loving. This charade blankets her real life, where a guilty conscience is non-existent and she lives only to fulfil her own inner desires for self-satisfaction, no matter what the cost to others." Sandy looked over at Strain for his reaction.

He was quick to jump in with his own version of summing up, "So, a female Nutter dressed in a suit, is that what you are telling us, Miss Moore?"

Holding his gaze and remaining positive she replied with, "If you think about what I have told you, then you will find it easier to get inside the head of the murderer. Maybe you will start to understand how they think. Although in all honesty, probably only a sociopath really knows how another sociopath thinks or what makes them tick, but you can give it a try. We can all be trained to think differently, and it will be hugely beneficial for you to learn this skill."

"Okay," said Rob. "I think that's really interesting and it's got me thinking." He looked over at Strain who was rolling a pencil through his fingers with a disinterested look on his face. "What if I go to the local gyms, Guv? There are only two in town; I could check out their members list, narrow it down to females aged around thirty and check out their fitness routine and how regularly they go. Maybe even join them. It wouldn't be the worst assignment I've ever had. Even if one of them does turn out to be a murderer."

Strain thought for a moment, ran his fingers through the top of his hair and sighed. "Yes, why not. At this point in the investigation we have nothing better to go on. Once you've established yourself, go jogging and see if any of them you have seen at the gym also appear outside of the gym."

"Will do, Guv." He turned to Sandy. "Thanks, you've given me some inspiration."

"You're welcome," she said, relieved that Rob had taken the lead.

She closed her file, picked up her brief case and without looking at Strain she left the room.

"What a load of rubbish," Strain said as he got up to fetch himself a coffee.

CHAPTER THIRTY-THREE

Despite Strain's unwillingness to indulge Sandy Moore's profile, Rob, was totally inspired, and it was just the tonic he'd needed to renew his flagging enthusiasm in the case. That and the added bonus of being able to hang out at the gym as part of his working day, had cheered him up no end. He was also pleased at the prospect of being out of Strain's way for the foreseeable future. His boss was a faultfinder most of the time and Rob needed to do something positive, so he was full of confidence as he took on his new role.

It meant he was making an earlier start in the morning and finishing later in the evening, but initially he enjoyed it. As his fitness levels rose, and he got to know the people that attended the gym, he realised that he personally was probably the only one who was benefitting from this undercover work, and not his case. His assignment was over in no time, and turned up, to use Strain's words, "Jack shit."

The failure of his assignment at the gyms had taken its toll on Rob's mental health. He had failed to generate any new leads and it had made him question his ability as a Detective, and he hit an all-time low. He was seriously considering asking the Chief Supt for a transfer. He began to feel negative, and he had no idea how any murders ever got solved. It was like doing a thousand-piece jigsaw when at least eight hundred of the most important pieces were missing, and he was even beginning to understand why Strain was tetchy most of the time. There appeared to be no job satisfaction in this line of business. Nevertheless, he did continue with the jogging and here he was at roughly seven o clock on a damp and dreary morning doing just that, jogging through the local woods.

It baffled him why anyone would want to do this activity on a daily basis. it was certainly not his idea of a fun exercise. There was little or no interaction with people because most of them had earphones clipped to their ears and were engrossed in listening to their music, so consequently fellow joggers simply nodded their heads in acknowledgement as they passed by him. He used his jogging time to collect his thoughts and right now he was thinking back to the date he'd had with Sophie a few nights ago.

It had been some time since he had been out with a girl on a regular basis, and he had almost forgotten how nice it was getting to know someone. It hadn't taken them long to find out that they had a lot in common and they spent their time talking and laughing together. It was a pleasant distraction from his job, and he hoped that she was enjoying herself as much as he was. Stuart, one of his mates, was having a housewarming party the following week, and he was going to ask Sophie if she would like to go with him. Stuart and his wife, Penny, had moved about forty miles away towards Winchester, so it would mean an overnight stop, he hoped Sophie would be up for that too.

His thoughts returned to his jogging routine. He had done the same route twice a day and had only seen two people on a regular basis, neither of them, in his mind, had the making of a serial killer.

As he reached the top of the hill he stopped briefly and unclipped his water bottle and swigged a much-needed drink, then he took a right turn, but before he could begin the last leg of his run, he was startled by a familiar voice.

"Hello, Sergeant."

Bloody hell.

He looked at the person who was standing in front of him. "Hello," he replied. "I don't know whether I am more surprised to find you out jogging or the fact that you have spoken to me. I thought you hated me."

"I don't hate you. I was just upset and angry with the whole situation. I realise now that you were only doing your job and I apologise for being so rude to you," said Sherry Taylor.

"No harm done" Rob said, "I didn't have you down as a jogger though."

She laughed: "Me neither. And to be honest I never have been before, but since I have given up work, I've noticed a few pounds sneaking on and around my waistline, so I thought I'd give it a try. And actually, I'm quite surprised to find I'm rather enjoying it. It gives me a sense of freedom somehow. I can't explain it. But you, Sergeant Wilding, I would never have guessed that it would be something that you did in your spare time." As she spoke her gaze strayed up and down his body.

She's checking me out.

"Ah, well," he said. "It just shows that you never know till you know."   He was eager to turn the conversation back to her. "So is this your regular route? It's a wonder I haven't bumped into you before now?"

"To be honest, I'm a bit of a fine weather jockey; the slightest hint of rain and I'm more than happy to stay on the sofa!" Then with a quizzical tone to her voice she somehow managed to turn the conversation back to him: "So, come on, spill, is this jogging part of an investigation or is it genuinely something that you do regularly?"

"Oh absolutely it's what I do." Rob lied easily.

"Excellent. Maybe I'll bump into you again then." And she continued on her way."

He stood there for a few moments and watched her as she disappeared out of sight.

Fucking hell, I can't believe it. She's put herself right back in the frame.

He took a short-cut back to the car park and sat in his car for a few minutes. He finished off the rest of his water before driving to the station to tell Strain his news.

"So what do you reckon, Guv?" Rob asked anxiously, still clad in his sports attire.

"Well, she certainly keeps cropping up where you least expect her to. She's like a bad penny, and I reckon she's involved somewhere along the line. We just need to find out where. Keep up with the jogging, see if she turns up again."

"Will do." Rob replied, as he went off to the men's locker room to get changed.

As he fixed his tie and slipped on his jacket he felt pleased that his idea to put himself out there, was at last, beginning to pay off. On his way back to the office he saw Sophie in the corridor and he stopped to chat for a few minutes. He mentioned to her about his mates' party, and she had eagerly responded with a 'yes'. They stood chatting until they heard Strain bellow out loud how there must be some kind of drought, as his cup was bone dry.

CHAPTER THIRTY-FOUR

Strain rolled over in his bed. The urge to stay asleep this morning was strong. Five weeks had passed by since the last murder and a lot longer since he had seen Christie. Without a phone number or an address, he had no way of contacting her. He had hooked up with a couple of women during her absence from his life, but they were just one-night stands, and he had no interest in seeing either of them again.

His head felt thick and heavy from an overdose of whisky that he had enjoyed the night before. He had gone out in the hope that he might bump into Christie, but there was no such luck. He had no idea what was so different about this woman compared to any of the other women he had previously dated, one thing was clear though, he had fallen for her. He slung the duvet back, got out of bed and headed for the shower. The hot water worked its magic on his body, awakening his senses and it felt good as he stood there and let it gush over him. When he'd had enough, he grabbed a towel, tied it tightly around his waist and went into the kitchen, he flicked the switch on the coffee maker and left it to do its job.

He walked back into the bedroom and sifted through his wardrobe, smart dress was required today so he chose a blue Versace suit, shirt, and tie. He stood in front of the mirror and nodded his approval to himself.

The strong Americano coffee gave him the hit he needed to kick start his brain and he picked up the bulging folder from off the breakfast bar. He glanced through its contents and checked that everything he needed was in there. He was due in court at 10 a.m. to verify an arrest on one of his previous cases. Nailing the bastards was his favourite part of the job. He closed his front door and took the stairs down to the main entrance of his apartment block. The cold air felt refreshing on his face as he walked over to his car.

Although the traffic was heavy, the drive to the courthouse was uneventful and as luck would have it, he managed to find a parking space that was less than a ten-minute walk away. As he approached the building, he walked towards the concrete steps that led up to the grand entrance and stopped to light a cigarette. He wasn't a regular smoker, but he did enjoy the odd one or two now and then. He stepped on the butt and walked up the steps and through the double doors where he registered his arrival with a middle-aged woman at the reception desk. She checked him in and told him which courtroom his case was being heard in and he briskly made his way to court room three as she had instructed him.

At 10 a.m. sharp the collection of people who were standing in the waiting room were herded through into the courtroom by the usher. The case began and Strain listened in earnest. He was particularly interested in what the various witnesses had to say. Although he wasn't giving evidence, it was a case he had assisted with, and it was always good to see the outcome first hand. It would be another one to add to his collection.

He kept a journal of all the cases he worked on. The dates, and the verdicts, and had done since he'd first joined the force, and he would continue to do so, until he left or retired, whichever came first.

He watched avidly as the defence and prosecution battled it out for a victory, they were going hell for leather at each other, which in itself, Strain found entertaining, although he did have issues with the defence counsel. He couldn't comprehend how they managed to sleep at night or how they could live with the knowledge that they had helped to release a murderer or a rapist to freedom. Their victories often allowed a criminal to live amongst the weak and the vulnerable, almost certainly to commit their crimes again.

Snapped from his thoughts by the sound of his name being called, he got up and walked with an air of confidence over to the stand. He was sworn in and confirmed to the Prosecutor that he had been the arresting officer. He was not cross-examined because it was only verification that the correct procedure had been adhered to, and that was all that was required from him on this occasion.

Finally, the court adjourned for lunch and Strain made his way to the cafeteria. This was not open for public use but because of his status he was allowed to use it. He got himself a cup of coffee and a sandwich and found a vacant table in the corner of the room. As he finished off his sandwich and washed it down with his hot drink, he watched the barristers come and go. Some were eating whilst at the same time making notes for their files. He never tired of people watching. Then he saw someone, who, he never in a million years would have expected to see. "You have got to be kidding me," he said under his breath. A familiar face was smiling at him as she weaved herself through the crowded tables and across the room towards him.

"Hello Strain!" She said.

As he gazed in amazement at the barrister, who was standing in front of him fully wigged and cloaked, he couldn't keep the surprise out of his voice. "Christie!" He hesitated for a moment "I didn't know. We didn't discuss it."

"It never came up," she said, matter-of-factly, as she sat down opposite him. "May I join you?"

"Of course," he stammered slightly, as his natural composure was shaken and disappeared. She had wobbled him for a moment. "I had no idea," he said, failing to keep the annoyance out of his voice. "I wish you had told me!" The muscles in his face felt tight.

"Why? What difference would it have made?" She put her hand on his and said: "We are still going to have a great time together whether you know I'm a barrister or not. Anyway, you know now."

"That's not really my point." He felt deflated as if he already knew the answer to his next question. "So which side do you bat for? Prosecution or defence?"

"Defence," she replied and held his gaze as she took a sip of her coffee.

Strain felt the muscles in his face tense up even more. He didn't think this moment could get any worse. He was lost for words, which, in all honesty was possibly a first for him.

"Look, Strain, I'm sorry you feel so strongly about the fact that I didn't divulge my day job. If you feel I owe you some kind of an explanation then here it is and I don't mean to stand on my soap box, but I am very proud of who I am and what I do. I am also a party girl and experience has shown me that the mere mention of what I do all day can be a killjoy, you of all people should identify with this. I just like to socially escape from the serious side of my life. It's really no big deal."

A story whipped up in the true style of a barrister who has only minutes to think up a reply in order to placate a judge and jury.

He wanted to shout at her, 'actually it is a big deal', but instead he made no comment.

The silence between them was loud and clear.

"So how have you been?" She asked, trying to get past the obvious fact that he was still cross with her.

"Oh, you know, same old shit, different day. And you?"

"Yes, I'm okay thank you. I've just been so busy lately. My life has been totally consumed by my current case. In fact, it has taken over my life for several weeks now, so I haven't been up to much else."

She rubbed her leg against his under the table. "Have you missed me?" She asked him in a seductive voice.

"Yes, very much," he replied, shuffling on his seat.

"I'm really hoping for a verdict in the next couple of days, maybe we could hook up at the weekend?"

"Maybe," he said, and then quickly changed his mind and his attitude. He relaxed and smiled at her. "Yes, that would be great." He looked at his watch and suddenly realised that he had almost over-run his lunch break and there were only a few minutes to go before his courtroom resumed. "I've got to go," he announced in a disappointed voice as he got up and pushed his chair in.

"Okay," she said, flashing him a smile. "I'll see you in your local on Friday night."

"I'll look forward to it," he said trying to tear his eyes from hers. He wanted to kiss her, but he knew that would be inappropriate. "Bye," he said and swiftly returned to courtroom three wondering how the hell she managed to look so good dressed in a wig and gown.

He took his seat, ready for the rest of the hearing but it was fair to say that he had absolutely no idea what went on during the remainder of the trial, so it was a good job when a guilty verdict was delivered.

Strain left the building in a hurry and drove back to the station. Needing to expel some nervous energy he skipped past the lift and went up the stairs instead. In the office he found Rob making notes.

Rob looked up. "Hey Guv, how'd it go?"

"All good, we got a guilty verdict."

"Good job then. So what's eating you?"

Strain was surprised at Rob's observation and thought for a moment, not sure whether to keep his discovery to himself, and then walked over to Rob's desk, he needed to share his days' findings with someone and he knew he could trust Rob. "Okay then, cop a load of this and tell me what you think."

Rob sat up straight in his seat and looked directly at him.

"Christie, my elusive girlfriend, was at the courthouse today."

"On trial?"

"No, I almost wish she had been. You're not going to believe this because I'm not sure I do. She's a barrister."

Rob raised his eyebrows as he said, "You have got to be joking!"

"No, I'm not. I saw her and had a coffee with her in the courthouse cafeteria. She was wigged and gowned, a defence lawyer, none the less!"

Rob pulled a face as he said. "Your favourite type then. I can't believe she didn't tell you."

"Me neither but she didn't, she never said a word about it, and I didn't have the slightest inkling." He went quiet. "To be honest I feel a bit stupid, I mean, what sort of Detective am I, not knowing that the woman I've been sleeping with is as high up the legal chain as I am. It's days like this that I question my career choice."

"Bit fucked up," said Rob.

"More than a bit. I feel like she's been laughing at me all this time because she knew I was a Detective, and I didn't know anything about her."

"Maybe she had a good reason for not telling you. Has it put you off seeing her again?"

"No, it hasn't put me off, but it has made me wary. I'm meeting her on Friday night, so I'll have a chat with her then. Anyway, enough about my private life, have you caught my murderer yet?"

"Honestly, Guv, I'm stumped, we all are."

Strain sat down at his desk and put his feet up. After what he had just shared with Rob, he found himself thinking about Christie and how he felt about her being a defence lawyer. It was finally starting to dawn on him that their relationship was doomed. In the beginning it had been the intrigue that had turned him on the most, but as the reality began to unwind it was starting to have the opposite effect. He turned back to Rob. "Let's get the team together and thrash this through, see if we can find something we've all missed."

"Will do" said Rob, and he left the office.

CHAPTER THIRTY-FIVE

Holly Jones finished delivering her late-night news broadcast and handed the programme over to the weather reporter. She left the studio floor and took the lift down to her office where she slumped onto her chair and yawned. She let out a moan as she spotted the heap of paperwork on her desk that needed her attention. She stretched her neck and rotated her shoulders before beginning to rummage through the stack that had been added to by various people during the course of the day. In the middle of the pile, she came across a note to call a DCI Strain and a number to ring him back on. It wasn't marked urgent, and it was late, so she decided she would call him in the morning. She picked up the note and popped it into her handbag. Once she was satisfied that there was nothing else particularly important pending, she scooped the remainder of the paperwork together and put it all into her top drawer. She looked at her watch. It was 11.30 p.m. and she still had things to finish off. She could think of better ways to spend a Thursday night.

Why is there always so much to do and so many loose ends to tie up on the run-up to a holiday?

She was grumbling to herself and sighed as she cleared the rest of her desk, locked the top drawer, and left the office. She said goodnight to Frank, the night security officer, as she walked over to the lift.

"Goodnight, Holly, see you tomorrow."

She stopped and turned to face him. "Actually, no you won't. As from this very minute I am on annual leave for the next ten days. So, unless any tragedies occur and I get called in to cover it, my plan is to do absolutely nothing. And to be honest, as much as I love my job, I can't wait!"

She could see that Frank looked pleased for her as he asked, "Do you want me to escort you down to your car?"

Such a gentleman.

"No thanks, Frank, I'll be fine." She stepped into the lift and pressed the button.

The doors closed and it jolted into life ready to take her down to the ground floor. After a few seconds, the lift stopped, and the robotic voice announced the arrival to the lower level of the car park. As the doors opened, she began rummaging through her handbag for her car keys. She walked across the underground car park humming a tune out loud. It was eerily silent except for the sound of her tune and the noise of her high-heeled shoes as the clip-clop echoed through the parking lot.

She hated it down here. Even though it was well-lit, it still gave her the creeps. She thought about Frank's offer to walk with her and momentarily wished she had said yes, because when you are walking on your own, there is always just 'something' about the stillness of an underground car park.

She swung around abruptly, having scared herself, to find that, not surprisingly, there was no one following her. She laughed to herself at her silliness.

She had finally found her keys and as she approached her car, she pressed the button on the fob and her black Mercedes sports lit up. She opened the door ready to slide onto the grey leather seat and take her place behind the wheel. She had no idea what had hit her as she fell to the ground.

CHAPTER THIRTY-SIX

Holly opened her eyes, squinting, as she struggled to focus. She felt sick from the intense pain that was pounding inside her head and her arms were hurting. Her confusion was overwhelming as she tried to recall what might have happened to her. After what seemed like a few minutes, she realised that her arms were hurting because they were tied tightly behind her back and her ankles were also tied together. Some kind of tape was plastered firmly across her mouth, and she was struggling to breathe through her nose as she tried to take in her surroundings. Unfortunately, it was too dark to see anything. She felt very cold and confused as she lay there on the hard concrete floor. She dug deep into her memory, but it was hazy and unclear, the last thing she could remember was saying goodnight to Frank at work and taking the lift down to the car park. After that, her mind was a complete blank. Tears stung her eyes and crept down her face and she began to shake uncontrollably until eventually she passed out.

She woke up with a start as what felt like a hard slap hit her face. She could barely see, partly due to the dim light, and partly because her eyes were swollen from crying. The duct tape was still firmly in place and it muffled any sounds she tried to make. Just then a woman's voice came out of the darkness. Holly took in a sharp breath up her nose and momentarily held onto it.

"So you think I am insecure and attention seeking. Is that correct?" The woman's voice was calm and steady. "Please feel free to shake your head if you think I am wrong, but that was the opinion you chose to share with the world, wasn't it?"

Holly lay there frozen with fear as she listened to her captor. Suddenly a light so bright that Holly thought her eyes would explode was shining directly at her, burning through her iris's like a gas torch. She blinked profusely, but she remained blinded.

"Well now, Miss Holly bitch Jones, I can just about see from the look in your eyes that you may be a little bit sorry you said that now, and I plan to show you just how wrong you are."

Holly was struggling to make sense of this woman's words. She wanted to shout, 'who are you? and what do you want with me?' Then she realised, and bile rose up from her throat and filled her mouth. This was the serial killer. The murderer was a woman.

A sick laugh rang out and filled the air.

"Nobody will ever find you. Do you hear me? You will rot away in here on your own. Hardly the work of an attention seeker, wouldn't you agree."

At that precise moment Holly would have agreed to anything if it meant saving her life. But deep down she knew this was her end. She let out a muffled sound as she swallowed back the vile liquid that had risen and collected in her mouth, and she began to shake as she listened to her perpetrator's footsteps walking away from her, followed by a door closing and a key being turned, locking her into her own private hell.

She lay there in the dark, struggling to understand how this could have happened to her. Surely someone would find her. She couldn't die here. Not like this.

She whimpered as the tears began to stream uncontrollably down her face. Rapidly turning into hysterical sobs that were blocked from escaping by the tape that secured her mouth. And although her head still thumped with pain, a numbing sensation was slowly beginning to creep its way up through her body.

She tried to move her legs, but she was so cold, that she could no longer feel them. It was the same with her arms as she tried to wriggle them out of her restraints. She had no idea how long she had been like this, but eventually her pain was slowly being replaced with numbness. In a strange way she felt grateful, and as it spread through her body, she began to feel warmer. She was the most scared she had ever been in her life. She couldn't scream, and she couldn't move, she just lay there as her normally sharp mind pondered silently over her life. She thought about all that she had achieved, and also the things that clearly, she would now, never achieve.

Holly was not a religious person, yet she found herself reciting the Lord's Prayer over and over in her mind until finally she lost consciousness.

CHAPTER THIRTY-SEVEN

When Strain arrived for work that morning, he could see from the corridor that Sergeant Claire Redding from the missing persons unit was sitting there waiting for him in his office. They had dated briefly, the previous year and even though it hadn't worked out for them personally, they had managed to maintain a professional relationship.

"Morning Sir," she stood up as he joined her.

"I thought you might like to take a look at this report. It was filed yesterday but it only came to my attention this morning." The young Sergeant handed him the folder that she had been holding and Strain took it from her.

"What is it?"

"It's Holly Jones, Sir, the news reader that pissed off your serial killer. She's been reported as missing. She hasn't been seen by anyone for the last twelve days. Her boss has tried calling her, but she doesn't pick up. Her supervisor has visited her home address but there was no reply there either. They have checked out her social media page, and there has been no activity on her Myspace page since her last afternoon at work. Apparently, she was due back in the office two days ago after taking annual leave, but she never showed up. Her work colleagues all agree this is totally out of character and they are very concerned. So, I thought you might want to take a look."

"Yes, I do. Thank you. And well done for spotting the potential link with our serial killer, Sergeant," Strain said as he sat down and with a heavy heart began to read the report.

She nodded her head to Rob as she passed him coming through the door as she left the office. He had two cups of coffee and he handed one to Strain.

"Listen to this," Strain said, and he read it out loud. "Holly Jones was last seen at around 11.30 p.m. twelve days ago by Frank Hedges, who is the night security officer at Local Network News. Apparently, she left the office to start annual leave and hasn't been seen since. I left her a message about two weeks ago to call me, but I never heard back from her, and now I know why." Strain looked Rob directly in the eye and with a grim face he said, "Fuck, Rob! Our killer's got her. Come on." And he threw the car keys to him.

The local Network News offices were just a few miles out, on the other side of town, so it didn't take them long to get there. They entered through the Victorian style double doors at the front of the building, which gave it a false sense of grandeur. Inside the building there were several floors housing the different departments, but the main journalist office was on floor three. It was one large open-plan room, housing about sixteen desks. Each one was occupied.

After talking to some of Holly's colleagues, it was established that she was ambitious and had not let the grass grow under her feet, earning herself a seat on live TV. She had loved her job and all of her colleagues confirmed that she would never have voluntarily missed a day. They spoke to Frank Hedges, the night-watchman, who was possibly the last person to have seen her and he confirmed that there was nothing unusual or different about her mood that night. In fact, she had seemed to be in a good frame of mind; upbeat and looking forward to having some time off.

Strain noticed that Frank had a tortured look on his face as he spoke about her. It was as if he felt guilty about her disappearance, instantly suspicious Strain probed further, which revealed that Holly's decline of an escort from him to walk her to her car had left him feeling full of regret. He felt now that he should have insisted and if he had, then maybe he would have spotted something important or not quite right, and things would be different. Strain took a moment to reassure him that was most certainly not the case and a simpler explanation for her disappearance was still plausible.

Rob took a full list of her work colleague's names and said he would be in touch with each of them individually within the next forty-eight hours. He instructed them all to keep quiet about this investigation for the time being until they knew exactly what it was they were dealing with. He knew, given their vocation that this was like asking them not to breathe, and to be honest, he fully expected someone to leak the news, but they needed to try and keep it under wraps for now.

Strain and Rob left the offices and headed over to Holly's home address and after a short drive to the market town of Ringwood - on the outskirts of the New Forest - they pulled up outside the block of flats where Holly Jones lived. It had security gates at the entrance which were opened by the letting agent once Strain had identified himself. Rob had contacted the agent earlier on and after briefly explaining why they needed to gain access, he had agreed to meet them there with a spare set of keys, which he reluctantly said they could hang onto for as long as they needed to. Rob parked the car and the agent handed over the keys. Before he left, he showed them the allocated parking space for Holly Jones, which was empty.

"That's a bit strange Guv," Rob said. "Maybe she has gone away after all."

The small one-bedroom flat was neat and tidy and there were no signs of a struggle or a break-in. Both Strain and Rob were satisfied that Miss Jones's flat was not the scene of any crime, even so they spent just over an hour there looking through her various drawers and cupboards, finding nothing untoward. Rob did, however, find Holly's passport in the side pocket of a travel bag stored in her wardrobe.

"Well, Guv," he said, holding it up to show Strain. "She's obviously not away on an exotic holiday!"

"Mores the pity," Strain said. "Come on, there's nothing here for us."

They locked up and took the stairs back outside to the car park. As they were walking to their car, Strain's mobile rang. His face tightened and he gritted his teeth. "You have got to be joking? The dozy idiots. Okay, we're on our way."

"What is it, Guv?"

"You are not going to believe this, Rob, we've got to go back to the Network offices. They've just gone and discovered Holly Jones's car is parked in the car park. Idiots. You'd expect more from journalists." As he pulled the car door shut, he thought about Frank Hedges.

The forensic team were already there when they arrived on the ground floor and had cordoned off the area where her car was parked. They had already established that the car was clean. It seemed like she hadn't made it inside, as the vehicle was unlocked and the door was not closed properly, indicating that she had been attacked before getting into her car. They had found a small amount of blood splatter on the concrete floor at the side of the driver's door and a sample had been taken away for DNA testing.

Strain shook his head: "I can't believe that her car has been parked here for the last two weeks and nobody has even noticed! It must be a very lonely life being a news journalist."

They finished at the crime scene and returned to the office. The DNA result from the blood splat was made a priority and it was confirmed that it did indeed belong to Holly Jones. But that was all they got from the crime scene. Whoever had abducted her had been very careful not to leave any trace evidence behind.

Strain was standing in front of the incident board. He had added Holly Jones to the puzzle, although doubtful, he did wonder if she might still be alive. He couldn't believe that the network offices didn't have CCTV in the car park. Apparently, the powers that be hadn't thought it was necessary, because only the staff could access it and they did this either through the offices or with a key fob that remotely opened the entrance onto the road. Strain hoped in light of this event they would now consider reversing their decision. He had sent Rob to check out the closest CCTV cameras in the area. These were found to be located at the far end of the road where there were a couple of popular night clubs and generally more traffic activity from the main roundabout. He hoped by tracking the car owners seen around the time that Holly Jones had finished work, they might just get lucky and pick up on a lead.

Strain's thoughts were disturbed by the appearance of Sandy Moore, and as he looked over at her, he failed to hide his disinterest.

"You know you won't find her, don't you, Sir?" She said.

"And what makes you so certain of that, Miss Moore?" he asked, with a raised eyebrow.

"Well, it's quite obvious to me that your killer is proving a point. Holly Jones called your killer an attention seeker. What better way to prove her wrong? No news coverage, no attention, no anything. It's as simple as that."

"Anything else you would like to add, Miss Moore?"

"No, not at this moment" and she turned and left his office.

Strain let out a sigh and pursed his lips together, he hadn't meant to be rude to her, but he just couldn't help himself. She bought out a defensive side in him, but whether he liked her or not, what she had just said to him, made perfect sense.

He sat down and with his elbows on the desk he rested his head on his hands. He found himself wondering what sort of fate Holly Jones had endured or was still enduring.

His mobile rang and the name, Chief Superintendent Ridley filled the screen. "Sir," Strain said as he answered it. "Yes, right away."

Of course the chief wanted to see him. Could this day get any worse?

CHAPTER THIRTY-EIGHT

Christie walked into the pub, ordered herself a Bacardi and coke and found a vacant table in the far corner of the room, where she knew she would have a good view of the entrance door. All week she had been feeling really bad about Strain and the fact that she'd had to stand him up last weekend. She knew she was already on thin ice with him, but it had been unavoidable and was just so typical of her life. She was one hundred percent dedicated to her job and once she was involved in a case everything else had to take a back seat as she lived and breathed it until it was done and finished with. It was unfortunate that this particular case had gone on a lot longer than she had anticipated, the prosecution had produced an unexpected witness, and she'd had a huge folder of additional notes to process. So, although she didn't expect Strain to come in tonight, she had popped in anyway just on the off chance that he might make an appearance.

Every time someone walked through the door, she looked up to see if it was him. It had been a long time since she had liked a guy this much, probably as long ago as High School, but there was something about Strain that appealed to her, and she was reluctant to let go of him. But at the same time, she had huge commitment issues, or maybe it was trust issues. She wasn't sure what the difference was, if any. Her therapist had said that both these words were linked, and if you weren't able to trust then it followed that you wouldn't be able to commit.

She understood what she had been saying to her during their weekly, one-hour sessions and she didn't want to give up on having a life and falling in love, but her past constantly haunted her, which is why she kept messing up. Hopefully, Strain liked her enough to put up with her incessant ability to keep shying away.

CHAPTER THIRTY-NINE

Strain was glad to see the back of this shitty day. He'd had a lecture from Ridley, his Supt, for not being any closer to solving the murders. Even though he had potentially linked the disappearance of Holly Jones to the murder case, it hadn't involved good police work, but had simply been an obvious connection.

It was the same old story day in day out. This person that they were hunting, was good. He left them no clues and nothing to go on. Strain had, in no uncertain terms, been ordered to remove his head from his arse and work more closely with the profiler, Sandy Moore. He hadn't argued back, instead he'd nodded his agreement and exited the Superintendent's office before he said something that he might later regret.

Strain arrived home late after his shift, tired and sweaty. He headed straight for the shower, and after washing the days grime away, he grabbed a towel, dried off and tied it around his waist. With a scotch in one hand and the remote in the other he put the telly on and crashed on the sofa. Nothing grabbed his attention so he switched to a music channel and lay on the sofa looking up at the ceiling and inevitably not many minutes later he fell asleep. He woke up feeling cold and hungry, so he hauled himself off the sofa, got dressed and headed for his favourite Indian takeaway. There was a forty-five-minute wait until his order would be ready, so he crossed the road and took the five-minute walk to his local. As he pushed through the swing doors an abundance of loud conversation and laughter greeted him, he made his way to the bar and nodded to the barman.

"Looks like you've had a rough day" the barman said in a sympathetic tone, as he handed him a Scotch and water.

"Yeah, just a bit," Strain replied.

"Here, this may or may not cheer you up." He handed Strain a folded piece of paper.

"What's this?" Strain asked, as he looked down at the note.

"A woman left it for you earlier on this evening. I think she's gone now but I have seen you in here with her before."

"Cheers mate," Strain said as he glanced around the room. He held his glass up, took a swig, and then read the note.

If you can forgive me for not showing up last week, call me, 0798555666, Christie xx

Strain let out a sigh of relief and smiled to himself, as he looked at the phone number. He stuffed the note into his coat pocket, finished his drink and left the pub. He collected his takeaway and walked home.

CHAPTER FORTY

Strain put the leftovers from his takeaway into the bin. He was feeling too idle to take the bag outside so he tied the top of it instead, hoping that would be enough to contain the odour. He opened a can of lager and sat back on the sofa. His head was messed up with the crimes that he couldn't solve, the woman he couldn't pin down long enough to have a relationship with and the nagging feeling in the back of his mind that something wasn't quite right. He didn't rate the profile that Sandy Moore had created for him on their murderer. In his opinion it could relate to anyone. He could even fit it to Christie, for goodness sake. He didn't believe that anyone could profess to know the workings of a psycho's mind, or anyone's mind, he didn't even know his own mind half the time.

He got up and took the piece of paper that the Barman had given him earlier, out of his coat pocket and dialled the number.

"Hello Christie. How are you?"

"Strain. Am I pleased to hear from you."

He could tell by the tone in her voice that she was, but his mood was sombre as he said, "I don't know - are you?"

"Yes, of course I am. Look, I know I've pissed you off on more than one occasion, and I'm sorry that I let you down last weekend, but we didn't exchange numbers and I couldn't call you at work, because that would be unprofessional. However, it looks like my ingenious plan worked. I must remember to buy that bar-tender a drink. Am I forgiven?"

"Maybe," he said, trying to sound more upbeat than he felt. "So, have you got any free time in the near future or are you too busy releasing criminals back into the world?"

"Ouch!" she said. "And you wonder why I didn't tell you what I did for a living. Let's not talk about work. I get the distinct impression you're not too keen on my day job."

"Hmm, you could say that. Okay, let's keep it strictly personal. When can I see you?"

"How about five minutes?" She laughed. "How do you feel about that?"

"I think I'd feel like I may have a stalker." Strain shuffled in his seat. He was desperate to be with her. "Okay then, do that."

Less than five minutes later, he heard his door bell. He opened the door and took in the sight of her. She looked stunning in a short, fitted cashmere dress and leather ankle boots. He was just about to pay her a compliment but before he could say anything her lips had found his and her tongue was teasing around inside his mouth.

They stripped each other bare and tumbled into the bedroom and stayed there until morning.

"Well, this is a first," Strain said, as he walked into the bedroom with two cups of coffee. "I've showered and made coffee and you are still here. Have you no place better to be this morning?"

"I always have somewhere to be," she said, choosing to ignore his sarcasm. "I'm making an effort here. This is me showing you that I'm sorry for screwing up!"

"You screw just fine," he said playfully, as he set the coffees down on the bedside table.

"Be serious. You know what I mean."

"Yeah, I do, I'm just kidding with you. But I have to go into the office this morning. There's a lot going on at the moment!"

"I can imagine. The disappearance of Holly Jones is a nasty business."

"Yes, it is. So, beautiful lady, get your ass out of my bed, and I'll see you later."

CHAPTER FORTY-ONE

Sandy Moore took in a deep breath and popped her head through the office door. She hated that Strain made her feel edgy and nervous and she certainly wasn't in the mood for any of his sarcasm this morning, so to find Rob standing in front of the incident board, studying it, on his own, was a welcome relief. "Morning, Rob. How's it going?" She asked. "Any news on Holly Jones?"

Rob turned to face her. "Hi, Sandy. No, nothing. There's a press release this afternoon, appealing for anyone who may have any information on her whereabouts, to come forward. It's been hard work keeping the press quiet for this long, especially as it's one of their own, but it's time to inform the public."

"Inform them of what?" Strain asked as he walked through the door.

"Morning, Guv. I was just telling Sandy, that the first press release on Holly Jones goes out today."

"Yes, that's right. I had a brief meeting with them yesterday. I thought I had told you." He sat down at his desk and picked up the steaming cup of coffee with his name on it and drank it.

Rob thought that his boss must have some sort of asbestos lining in his mouth. Strain's eyes met Sandy Moore's, and he nodded his acknowledgement to her. She gave him a tight smile as she vacated the office without commenting.

Strain looked over at Rob. "I knew this was the first detailed press release, but has there been any mention of her disappearance before today?"

"Not to my knowledge, why do you ask?"

"No reason," he replied, as he picked up a file off his desk, tucked it under his arm and left the office.

Rob sat down and began trudging through the pile of notes relating to their murder case. He felt he knew the content off by heart, but there could be something that he'd missed.

He set aside Holly Jones's case file because they had no body, so technically she was still a missing person. Although, he was sure her name would eventually be added to the list of murdered women. Just then a cup of coffee appeared in front of him. He looked up and was surprised to see Sophie standing there. "What have I done to deserve this?"

"Nothing," she said. "I just thought you might like one. I saw you sitting here on your own, engrossed in whatever it is you are reading. Have you found anything significant yet that might solve your case?"

"No," he sighed. "It's like looking for a needle in a haystack. In fact, I think that would be easier. At least we'd know what we were looking for."

"I feel for you. It must be so frustrating. Well, I guess I should let you get back to it," and she turned to walk away.

"Thanks again." He hesitated for a second, and then called after her. "Sophie, I'm not very good company at the moment, but once this case is over, maybe we could see more of each other?"

"I'd like that," she replied.

"Great," he said, and turned his attention back to his paperwork.

When he came across Sherry Taylor's statement, he thought about her. He hadn't seen her for a while. He was going to tell Strain that he didn't think the jogging was a worthwhile exercise anymore. He picked up her statement, it shouldn't even be in this pile. It was quite obvious that there wasn't a connection between the death of Mrs Johnson, and the other murders.

He was jolted back to reality by the sound of Strain's voice booming out He had been to see Chief Superintendent Ridley, and clearly, it had not gone well.

Strain entered the office and dumped the files down onto his desk then turned to Rob. "Did you tell anyone outside of work about Holly Jones's disappearance, or would anyone from our team have talked about it?"

"Of course not. Why?" He replied as he looked up at Strain.

"Do you think any of her work colleagues could have leaked it out to anyone?"

"Yes, I'm sure they could have, but I think that would be highly unlikely. She wasn't just a headline. She was their friend and colleague. They were on board with us straight away to keep it quiet. Why?"

Ignoring Rob's question, Strain said. "Go back to the Local Network Offices and speak to them all again. See if you can find the one who might have shared this information."

"Okay Guv, but why?"

After a few seconds of silence Rob continued in a louder tone. "You need to let me in. I'm working on this case too, but you never give me anything to go on. I'm used to team work. But I feel like you don't trust me."

Strain was taken aback by Rob's sudden outburst.

He ran his fingers through his hair and thought for a moment, then he closed the office door. He turned back to face Rob and in a quiet voice said, "I saw Christie last night and she knew about the disappearance of Holly Jones and even though I had a short meeting with the press office only yesterday, regarding the report, I didn't think anything of it until you said this morning that the first press release was today."

"So, what are you thinking?"

"Honestly, I don't know what to think. Let's check out option one and see if anyone has talked."

"Okay, er, just a thought. Shall I take Sandy Moore with me, seeing as this is her speciality? She might be able to spot something that I don't."

"Yes, that's a good idea,"

Strain took advantage of having a quiet moment. He couldn't believe he was even thinking this but was it possible that Christie might somehow be involved in his case. He took the profile that Sandy Moore had prepared for them out of the file and read it through once more. As he did so, certain words leapt up off the page and danced in front of his eyes.

Successful and professional.
Woman.
Sexual relationship when she needs them.
In control.

The list flagged up seemingly endless similarities to the woman.

"Oh, Christ," he said aloud, recalling his own summing up; a female nutter dressed in a suit.

He let out a sigh as he rubbed his twenty-four-hour shadow with his right hand. He was obliged to inform his boss regarding any potential conflict of interest, but he knew he would be taken off the case if Christie was investigated, and there was no way he wanted that to happen. So, for the time being, he needed to keep it quiet, whilst he conducted some background checks on the elusive woman. This would be difficult to do, and a lot to ask of Rob. He wasn't sure where to start. He couldn't go poking around at the courthouse, and he hadn't asked her which law firm she worked for. He didn't even know where she lived. "What a jerk," he muttered under his breath. Then he jumped up, grabbed his car keys, and made for the door. He'd left the coffee cups, unwashed, in the sink this morning. So maybe there was a way to find out more about her without her even knowing.

CHAPTER FORTY-TWO

Strain pulled out of the station car park and followed the slip road onto the dual carriageway. Looking ahead he could see that the roads were still quite busy, so he made use of his emergency vehicle lighting. With this on, it was easier to weave in and out of the moving traffic without causing alarm or being reported for dangerous driving. Twenty minutes later he pulled into his reserved parking space outside his apartment block and made a dash for the entrance doors. He didn't wait for the lift, instead he took the stairs two at a time. He was out of breath as he barged through his front door and into the kitchen. He had driven like a lunatic, although he didn't know why, it wasn't like he had a cleaner due in anytime soon, who might have washed any DNA or fingerprints down the sink. He took two evidence bags out of his pocket and with a gloved hand he carefully picked up the two used coffee cups from out of the sink. Luckily, he hadn't put them in soak. He placed one into each bag and sealed and labelled them. One was his and the other one had been used by Christie. After a more sedate drive back to the station, he headed straight down to the lab and personally handed the two mugs over to Ed, the pathologist who was in charge of everything that came through the lab doors. Strain asked him to run them for prints and DNA.

"Under no circumstances are you to give the results to anyone other than myself or Sergeant Wilding, is that clear?"

The tall thin man dressed in a white coat nodded his agreement. He had known Strain for a long time, so he was used to his frosty manner.

In the office, Rob and Sandy had just arrived back and were sitting down chatting. They jumped up from their chairs when Strain walked in, feeling like they had been caught skiving.

He looked directly at them. "Well?"

"Nobody has admitted to leaking any info, Guv."

Strain felt sick inside. This was not looking good. "Okay guys, thanks." He could see their disappointment as he sat down at his desk.

"What, is that it then?"

"For now." Strain replied, without looking up at either of them.

Rob walked out of the office behind Sandy and followed her over to the lift. "Thanks for your help today."

"No problem," she replied. "It's nice to finally be accepted."

Rob went back to the office. "What now then?"

Strain could tell he was pissed off. "Close the door."

Rob did as he was told.

"Look I'm sorry if that appeared rude. I didn't mean to be dismissive, but I just want to keep the details between the two of us for the time being."

"Oh, okay. Sorry, I didn't mean to jump to conclusions."

Strain nodded and continued speaking. "I went home earlier and got mine and Christie's coffee mugs that we used at breakfast this morning. I've taken them to the lab and Ed's going to try and squeeze them in as a matter of priority for me. Hopefully, we should have some info first thing in the morning. I've told him to only give the results to you or me. Are you all right with this, Rob?"

Rob nodded. "Of course, why wouldn't I be? I'm a bit confused though, what exactly do you think Christie's involvement is?"

"I'm not entirely sure, but the best outcome here is that the results will clear her from our investigation."

"I didn't realise she was a person of interest. When did that even happen?"

"It's mainly for my own peace of mind, Rob." It hadn't occurred to him that Christie moved in similar circles to him, and she could easily be privy to certain knowledge that had not yet been made public.

He looked at his watch. It was almost 6 p.m. "Right, I have to go up to the human resources office and sort out an appointment with Hilary to go through the list of new recruits, so you might as well have an early night. Depending on what the outcome of the results are, we might have a busy day tomorrow."

Rob fidgeted, using his thumb to roll his ring around his middle finger. He wasn't entirely sure that what his boss was doing was above board, but he nodded and said, "Okay, Guv."

CHAPTER FORTY-THREE

Strain's meeting with Hilary, in human resources had gone on longer than he had planned. He had only popped up to her office to arrange a time that would be convenient for them both to get together, but she had somehow wangled it that they ended up making a start.

When he eventually arrived home he went straight to the freezer and took out a small bag of ice. He dropped three cubes into a glass and poured a Scotch over it, swishing it around and knocking it back almost immediately. He poured another one and went into the lounge. He drank it a lot quicker than he'd meant to, but it was having the desired effect. He didn't know whether to call Christie or not. She would be expecting him to ring but he wasn't sure how he would be with her. On the other hand, if he did make the call, he might be able to find out where she was living. He poured himself yet another drink and dialled her number.

"At last," she said as she answered the phone, "I thought you'd forgotten me?"

"Christie. Hi, you knew it was me?"

"Oh yes. I saved your number yesterday. I have you labelled under 'sexy hunk'."

Strain gave a half-hearted laugh.

"Is everything okay?" She asked.

"Yeah, everything's fine. Busy day, that's all."

"That's definitely one of the down sides to our chosen careers. Of course, there is only one way to make sure the day ends well."

"Yes, I'm sure that's true but it will have to be later," he said in a cool tone "I have some stuff to sort out first, but if you give me your address, I'll come over to yours when I'm done." He held his breath as he waited for her response.

"Oh, okay," she said, hesitantly. "But if you don't mind it would be better if I come over to your place. My sister is staying with me for a few weeks so we wouldn't have the place to ourselves, which means that we would have to behave, and I'm not sure that we are physically capable of such a task." She let out an awkward laugh.

"Well I'd like to think there is more to our relationship than just the physical side," he replied. "I'm sure we can behave if we try. After all we are both adults. I could just call in for a cup of coffee."

"I've just told you Martin; my sister is staying with me so it's not convenient."

Her tone was stern, and he could hear the irritation in her voice. She had never called him by his Christian name before. His mind was racing, and he wasn't sure how to handle the situation, He knew if he pushed her harder, he would lose, and she could be totally innocent, and he might put their relationship at risk for no good reason.

He cleared his throat. "Okay, no problem. I'll give you a call when I've finished."

"Fine," Christie replied, and ended the call.

CHAPTER FORTY-FOUR

Christie chucked her phone down onto the sofa and sat there for a moment.

What the hell was that all about?

Feeling agitated she got up and paced up and down her lounge. Finally, she grabbed her jacket and bag and stepped out into the cold night air. She had no plan in mind but very quickly realised it was far too cold for a walk so she hopped on the first bus that came along. She recognised the route it was taking and got off close to Strain's local.

An hour or so later her phone rang and she watched as the name 'sexy hunk' flashed up on the screen. Ignoring the call, she switched her phone off and dropped it into her bag and turned to the barman. "I'll have another Bacardi and coke when you're ready please." She smiled at him. "You're new here aren't you? I'm quite sure I would remember if I had seen you before."

"Yes," he replied. "This is only my second week."

Christie watched as the drink gushed over the ice in her glass, and as he opened a bottle of coke and put them both down in front of her, she could see she was making him nervous.

"That's £5.70p please."

As she paid him the money, she allowed her hand to gently touch his. She looked at the name on his badge: "So, Tom, what time do you get off?" she asked in a low, sensual voice.

He looked at his watch before replying. "In about an hour."

"I'll be waiting in the car park for you," she said, and she could almost see him shiver as he silently nodded his answer.

Christie picked up her drink and found an empty table that was tucked away in a corner of the room. As she sat down, she looked over at the barman who was still staring at her as if he didn't believe what she had just said to him.

As she sat there enjoying her drink, she was approached at different times by a couple of men who fancied their chances with her, but she gracefully declined their advances. She felt pleased with herself for making the decision to come out; it was a better choice than the alternative, which was to have stayed at home brooding over Strain's pushy attitude. It was almost an hour later when she finished her drink and left the pub and not too long after that, the barman stepped out of the back door that led directly onto the car park.

She saw him look over at her, sitting in a taxi, and noticing his hesitation, she opened the window and beckoned to him to join her. No sooner had he sat down next to her she placed her hand on his thigh. "Your place or mine?" She could see that he was unsure, so without waiting for a reply she gave the taxi driver her address and they sped off into the night.

CHAPTER FORTY-FIVE

At 8.30 a.m., Rob greeted Strain with a grim face, a cup of coffee and a new case file.

"What's this?" Strain asked, as he took the file and the coffee, and using his foot he pulled his chair out from under his desk.

He sighed as he sat down. He could really do without this. He was still distracted by the events of the previous evening. He had called Christie half a dozen times before eventually giving up. It was obvious that he had annoyed her. But was it because he had been pushy or because she had something to hide?

Rob explained, "About twenty minutes ago, the body of a young white male was found."

"Is it a suspicious death?"

"Yes, he was found in Lakeland Woods by two Forestry Commission guys."

"Lakeland Woods, the first crime scene. Is it the same M.O?"

"No, it's not quite the same this time. Because like I just said, the victim is male, and he wasn't out jogging. But yes, you are right, Lakeland Woods was the first crime scene."

Strain didn't drink his coffee. He got straight up and walked back out of the office with Rob following closely behind him.

After a silent drive they arrived at the entrance to Lakeland Woods and showed their ID cards to the police officer who was standing in front of the blue and white tape, used to cordon off the area. He acknowledged both Strain and Rob, and after handing them each a pair of shoe covers and a pair of gloves, he lifted the tape for them both to pass underneath, allowing them to join the forensic specialists. Strain, now clad in forensic protection, made a beeline for the pathologist, although he was from the same team, it wasn't Ed.

"What have you got for us?"

"Not much yet, I'm afraid. We have the body of a young man, life extinguished roughly seven hours ago. There is evidence that he may have had sex before he died. It looks like he wore a condom, but it has been removed from the scene."

"How did he die?"

The pathologist knelt down by the victim's side. The body was lying face down and he pointed to his findings as he spoke. "My initial inspection shows a head wound here, at the base of the skull, possibly dealt by using a blunt object. However, I would say the actual cause of death was most probably by strangulation."

"Was he killed here or moved here post mortem?"

"I don't know that yet either, but I think it may be the work of your serial killer, and not just because strangulation appears to be the cause of death but there was a chiffon scarf covering his head. It's been bagged." He looked up at Strain as he said, "Your serial killers trade mark, I believe." He continued to speak as he got to his feet. "Obviously, I'll know more once I get him back to the lab. We'll run tests to check his alcohol level and the usual. So, if that's all, I'd like to get on. I'm ready to roll him over now."

Strain and Rob stepped to the side and the pathologist signalled to two other members of his team, who assisted him in moving the body into an open body bag and onto a stretcher.

"Do we know who he is? Have you checked his pockets. Was he carrying any ID?" Strain bent down to look at the victims' face, but before anyone could answer, Strain gasped. "Jesus Christ! I know him! That's Tom, the new barman at my local."

CHAPTER FORTY-SIX

They left the scene and drove back to the office.

"I have to admit that I'm struggling to understand here, just how Tom is involved and what on earth he might have done to end up being murdered by our serial killer. He hadn't worked at the pub for long, maybe a couple of weeks, tops. Rob I'm going to need you to go to The Golden Goose and take statements from the owner and anyone who was working there last night and get as many customers as they can name that were drinking in there. I'm quite sure they have CCTV and you won't have to rely on their memories. If they do, then bring the last twenty-four hours of footage back to the office and scrutinise it.

"Right Guv," but as Rob turned to leave, a man in a white lab coat entered the office. It was Ed. He closed the door behind him and walked over to Strain.

"Here's your info, mate," he said, and held out the folder for Strain to take, but then, changing his mind he opened it himself and started to read its contents out loud.

"These are the DNA results from the coffee cups that you gave me yesterday. Obviously one set of prints are yours and the other set of prints belong to a white female named Christie Harding." He looked over the top of his glasses at Strain before continuing. "Christie Harding was formally known as Christina Wells. She's a Barrister and one half of a pair of identical twins. There's a lot of info on her because of her status in the legal chain, she's very highly respected. However, the same can't be said of her twin sister, who was originally known as Tracy Wells. She is a paranoid schizophrenic and until about three years ago she was detained under the Mental Health Act." He paused momentarily for effect before continuing. "Tracy Wells murdered both of their parents when she was just ten years old and as a result of this, she was detained for her own safety as well as for the safety of others. Her sister Christina was placed in care with John and Shelia Harding - a couple who initially fostered her and later went on to adopt her - are both still alive and currently living in Southgate. Christie Harding is actually the person responsible for securing the release of her sister, Tracy, from Queen's Road Psychiatric Unit and placing her back into society, under her new name of Sherry Taylor."

Ed moved towards Strain, who was sitting there with an indescribable look on his face.

"Thanks Ed," Strain said taking the folder off him. He turned to face Rob, whose features were frozen with disbelief.

"What do we do now, Guv?"

Strain took in a long breath and pursed his lips together as he shook his head. "We don't do anything yet. We need to think about this carefully before we take any action. We've got Sherry Taylor, the Carer, alias Tracy Wells, a one-time murderer, and Christie Harding, the lawyer, who is protecting her sister and both of their identities. He rubbed his forehead. "I need time to think this through. So, carry on with what you were going to do, and get over to the Pub."

CHAPTER FORTY-SEVEN

Rob arrived back at the office four hours later, armed with statements, names, and CCTV footage. He put everything down on his desk and made for the coffee machine. He could see Strain standing at the far end of the corridor, talking to Hilary from Human Resources. They were deep in conversation, but he couldn't hear what they were saying. Rob got two coffees and after placing one on Strain's desk he sat down and tried to drink his own, but it was too hot, and he burned his tongue. He abruptly put it down again. He was feeling tetchy. Someone at the pub could have offered him a drink, it's not like they didn't have anything. He looked up as Strain came in, picked up the USB stick and gestured to him.

"How did you get on?" Strain asked, as he walked over and stood in front of him.

"I think you are going to want to see this!" He pushed the USB into his computer and pressed a few keys. Within seconds, images from The Golden Goose Inn filled the screen.

Strain moved around to stand next to Rob.

The recording commenced at 6.00 p.m., but because Rob had already watched it through, he was able to fast forward the footage to the different points of interest.

He stopped it at 9.00 p.m. and watched, barely breathing, as he waited for a response from Strain, as the recording showed a woman entering the bar. She walked over and sat on a high stool and ordered a drink. Now Rob had never met the infamous Christie, but the woman on the screen, although more glamorous, bore a striking resemblance to Sherry Taylor. Rob heard Strain catch his breath, but he remained silent. He stopped and started at the different stages of the footage which revealed that this woman was in the pub for a couple of hours and it was evident that she had been flirting with their latest murder victim, Tom Lewis. Eventually, she moved away from the bar area and sat at a table on her own for just over an hour before leaving at 11.00 p.m. Twenty minutes later, Tom, the bar tender, exited through the back door which led directly out on to the car park. The camera that covered the perimeter of the car park revealed that he got into a taxi.

"I have spoken to the taxi company, Guv, and the driver has confirmed that around 11.30 p.m. he took our victim and a woman fitting the description of the lady in the bar to the address I have written down in my pocket.

Strain's blood ran cold. "Fucking hell, Rob, that's Christie!"

"He also confirms that he was called back to the same address an hour and a half later, picked the man up and dropped him off, very much alive, at a popular Bistro Bar on New Road called, The Lantern." He heard Strain breathe out a sigh of relief. "So, you see, Guv, although she may have been unfaithful to you, at least we know she's not a murderer."

"I guess I should be thankful for small mercies." Strain said.

"I stopped off at the Bistro bar about an hour ago, but it was locked up. According to the opening times on the door, they open all night and close all day. I called both the emergency numbers that were listed on the licence board above the door, but no one answered either of them. I'll go back later and talk to them in the hope they also have CCTV cameras."

"Good work, Rob," Strain said sincerely, "you seem to have this well in hand. He walked over to his desk and picked up his coffee. Now let's get moving on the information that Ed gave us earlier. We need to bring in both, Sherry Taylor and

Christie for questioning and find out what is going on. "How the hell does a convicted murderer with a serious mental health disorder get to be a carer for the elderly." He shook his head as he added: "Sometimes our system stinks."

Rob nodded his agreement as he thought back to the fact that Sherry Taylor had murdered both of her Parents, a fact he was having trouble digesting. "How is this going to work, Guv?" he asked. "You know, with you being involved with Christie."

"I do not want to be taken off this case, but I don't want to screw it up either, so I'll interview Sherry Taylor, while you interview Christie Harding, then there's no conflict of interest."

Rob didn't feel entirely comfortable with the situation, but this was the best course of action for now.

"I have her address in my pocket from the taxi driver. Shall I go straight over there now?"

Strain glanced down at his watch "No, if I was you, I'd go to the courthouse first. Barristers tend to work long hours, so I think that's your best shot and if she's not there, then you can go to her home address. Keep me informed of your progress. Meanwhile I'll get a couple of uniform to meet me over at Taylor's house."

CHAPTER FORTY-EIGHT

Rob entered the court building and headed straight for the reception desk. He showed the young receptionist his warrant card and asked her who he needed to speak to in order to find out which Barristers were attending which court room today.

"I can help you with that," she said. "Who is it you are looking for?"

"Christie Harding."

She made a few moves with the mouse then pointed him in the direction of court four. He had a word with the security guard on the door, who conveyed the message to the court usher, then he took a seat and waited.

He saw Christie step into the corridor. Her lips were pursed as she walked over to him.

"Can I help you Sergeant?"

"I'm sorry to disturb you at work," he said, holding out his warrant card. "I'm Sergeant Wilding."

She felt irritated as she asked him, "How can I help you?"

"Is there a private room we could use? I need to talk to you regarding an on-going investigation. I think you may have valuable information to contribute."

Christie let out a sigh. She hated being disturbed at her place of work, but she didn't want to make a scene in front of her learned colleagues, and she most certainly didn't want to become the subject of whispers. Instead, she reluctantly offered a different solution. "Fine, but not here. I'll come to the station as soon as court is finished. Sometime between 5 and 6 p.m. Does that suit you?"

"Thank you, I appreciate that," and he handed her a card. "If you speak to the duty officer on your arrival, he will call me."

Christie took the card and turned and walked away without a second glance.

She found herself wondering if Strain would be part of this so-called talk. She was feeling rotten about her sex romp with the bar tender the night before. It had been cheap and dirty, and she was cross with herself for behaving like that. Even though she and Strain weren't exclusive, she felt like she had betrayed him, but she had always been impulsive. She went to the cafeteria to get a drink before court was recalled. She poured herself a chilled glass of water and started to read the headlines from one of the many newspapers that were readily available to them. As the shock of what she was reading crept up through her shoulders and rose steadily up to her throat, she thought she might be sick.

CHAPTER FORTY-NINE

Christie arrived at the Police Station later than anticipated. It was 7.15 p.m. Following her instructions, she reported to the duty officer at the front desk and Rob came down and escorted her into interview room two, and he indicated for her to sit down.

"Can I get you a drink of tea, or coffee?"

"No, thank you. If you can just tell me why I am here please, it's been a very long day. Is it regarding the murder of the young barman? Because I can assure you that he was very much alive when he left me, but I imagine you are already in possession of that information." She fidgeted slightly in her seat.

"No, it's nothing to do with the murder of 'Tom Lewis'."

She flinched at the sound of his name. After all, she had been to bed with this man less than twenty-four hours earlier and now he was dead, murdered. She stretched her shoulders slightly. "Then I would appreciate it if you would tell me what this is all about. I am more than a little intrigued as to how you think that I may be of assistance to you?"

As Rob sat down opposite her he could not believe the solid physical likeness between this woman and her sister. It was like sitting in front of Sherry Taylor and it took him a few minutes to gain his composure, he had to blink to break his stare. He opened a folder and asked, "Do the names Tracy Wells or Sherry Taylor mean anything to you Miss Harding?"

He could see her body deflate slightly and her eyes appeared to cloud over. "It's more than obvious to me that you already know the answer to that question,"

He had no intention of playing games with her. "Can you tell me what you know?" Rob asked gently.

"Probably as much as you do, Sergeant, but okay." She shifted in her seat and sat upright before she began to speak. "Tracy Wells is my twin sister and she's had extreme behavioural problems for almost her entire life, and it was quite apparent at an early age. I can remember that she had a lot of imaginary friends from as young as three years old, all of whom hated me. It wasn't until she started to become violent towards me that our parents realised that there was something a lot more serious going on, and it wasn't simply down to competitive twin behaviour like the Doctor had suggested, and more often my sister's deep and sinister side started to rear its ugly head. She began to lose control of her imaginary friends, or more precisely, as we later went on to discover, her hallucinations. These hallucinations were telling her to do dreadful things, and over a relatively short period of time she went from being somewhat rude and withdrawn to becoming aggressive, destructive, and dangerous." Christie shuffled in her seat. "I'm sorry, could I have a drink of water please?"

Rob indicated to an officer who was walking down the corridor and asked him to fetch her one. On his return, he placed the plastic cup of water down on the desk in front of Christie and she picked it up straight away and took a sip before continuing.

"Thank you" she said, and she took in a breath to compose herself while he left the room, closing the door behind him. "Our parents were terrified of her, and they wanted her to be sectioned. But before this could happen, the Doctor wanted her to undergo a series of tests to confirm her diagnosis. The system was slow, with little support back then, so, she still lived at home with us, as a family. Unfortunately, this proved to be a huge mistake, because in 1981, when my sister was just ten years old, she loaded my parent's tea with her sedatives and then hacked them both to death whilst they were asleep in their bed. Luckily, I was on a sleep over at a friend's house, or I may have suffered the same fate. Or maybe that was the reason she chose to do it then, knowing I wasn't there."

She hesitated briefly and Rob noticed that she shuddered as the memory unfolded. "I arrived home the following morning to find the bloodied massacred bodies of my parents, lying side by side in their bed and my sister sitting on the floor at the bottom of it, rocking backwards and forwards, and humming a lullaby. I was screaming hysterically but she didn't flinch. I ran from the house and stood on our driveway screaming until one of the neighbours came out to see what was wrong. It was only then that Tracy was detained in a psychiatric unit. A bit late, wouldn't you say, Sergeant? The police found a notepad in Tracy's room. She had planned it all out, written it all down, what she was going to do and what time she was going to do it. Apparently, it was meant to be a surprise for me."

Rob was listening intently to what she was saying and nodded solemnly.

She took another sip of water and continued. "Consequently, we were left orphaned, and with Tracy locked away, I was sent to live with foster parents, who later went on to adopt me. I consider myself to be lucky, Sergeant, because I went on to have a very happy upbringing, and, with a little help from something called 'Dissociative amnesia' - a condition in which a person cannot remember important information about their life - I somehow managed to completely forget about Tracy for the next fifteen years. But once I had qualified and went into practice, all that began to change. Maybe a case triggered something, or maybe my mind felt it was finally able to deal with the trauma of remembering - who knows - but I found myself, quite unexpectedly, starting to have flashbacks and nightmares. I began thinking about her. I did my own research into child schizophrenia." Christie shifted in her seat. "Did you know that it is twenty to thirty times more severe in children than it is in adults? The hallucinations tend to be more intense and more frightening with voices constantly telling them to do violent and evil things.

The more I read about my sister's condition, the more I began to understand her behaviour towards me. You know it really wasn't her fault. Apparently, it is difficult to treat because most of the antipsychotic drugs that work on adults do not work on children. It's a devastating fact, Sergeant, that the system didn't just let my parents down, it also let Tracy down. A quicker diagnosis could have prevented her from murdering our parents and might have resulted in her getting the correct medical help that she so desperately needed at that time."

She took a tissue from her pocket and dabbed at her eyes.

Rob didn't want to interrupt her, so he remained silent and let her compose herself.

"Five years ago, I went to see Tracy. And quite honestly, I was amazed by our likeness. The face that was looking back at me was mine and I had an overwhelming feeling to protect her, albeit eighteen years later. I felt a strong connection to her. They say that about twins, don't they? Anyway, I started to visit her once a week and she began to look forward to my visits, as did I. She seemed to be a totally changed person and behaved in a normal manner, even laughing, and joking with me. I felt I had finally got the sister I had always wanted. She had accepted her illness and fully understood that as long as she took her meds she could be as normal as the next person. It was a long road and took another two years, but I battled on and fought for her and finally, after twenty years of containment she was deemed fit to be released back into society. I had to play an active part in her readjustment programme, I even took an oath to be responsible for her. I also had to assure the authorities that I would visit her at least twice a week at her home and I was to report to them immediately with any changes that occurred for the worse, no matter how insignificant they seemed. A Doctor and a therapist were also appointed to her and were relegated to check on her once a fortnight. I changed her name. I thought it may help her to make a fresh start and she adjusted perfectly well to normal life. It wasn't long before she got a job with an agency caring for people. It was simply amazing how she took her new life in her stride and began to blossom in it. There was a blip about twelve weeks or so ago, when one of the old ladies in her care, whom she was very fond of, died, but she recovered from the ordeal very well." Christie took another drink. "So, there you have it, Sergeant, that's you completely up to date." She looked at him long and hard. "Can I ask you why you want to know about my sister?"

"I can't say too much yet, but I can tell you that we are bringing her in for questioning. Let's say she may know more about the death of the old lady, Mrs Johnson, than we first thought."

Christie's hand flew to her mouth, and she leapt to her feet. "I must see her. I need to be with her!"

"I'm afraid that's not going to be possible right at this minute, but I will let you know what is happening later."

He looked at her with kindness. He was thinking how different his own life could have been and how easily this silent disease could seep in undetected, unleashing its devastating effect on anyone.

As she turned to leave, she took a card out of her pocket and handed it to him.

He accepted the card. "Thank you for your time, you have been very helpful."

Rob remained seated in the interview room for about ten minutes after Christie had left. It had been an emotional interview. To look at Christie Harding - a respected Barrister – you would automatically assume that she had come from a privileged background and certainly not endured both her parents being murdered and her sister being locked away.

He gathered up his notes and made his way down to the other end of the corridor towards interview room one.

CHAPTER FIFTY

It had been a long and stressful afternoon for Strain which wasn't over yet. Due to certain events, he had only just begun his interview with Sherry Taylor. When they had initially arrived at Taylors' house earlier in the afternoon, she had refused to open the door. After some reassurances, she'd relented. Then, she'd refused to go with them voluntarily, which caused further complications. In the end Strain had lost his patience and he'd arrested her under suspicion of murder. His actions took its toll on her and she'd become dramatically unhinged. Snarling and screaming at them, so they'd had to handcuff her. This upheaval had resulted in further delays whilst they waited for Taylor to calm down until it was okay to question her. Strain had organised for a duty solicitor to be called in, but unfortunately, he took an hour to arrive, so there was more unscheduled waiting around before he could interview her.

Finally, with everything and everybody in their place, he could begin, or so he thought. There was a knock on the door and an officer entered and spoke quietly to Strain, who, with a look of disapproval on his face got up and left the room.

"This had better be good, Miss Moore?" he said as Sandy approached him.

"I'm sorry for the interruption DCI Strain, but I've only just heard that you have Sherry Taylor in for questioning.

"My apologies, Miss Moore. I didn't realise that I needed to keep you informed of my movements."

Ignoring his remarks, she said. "I wanted to offer you some advice, regarding how I believe, you should tackle her."

Strain's face muscles tightened: "Really?"

Without giving him time to walk away she said. "Don't go barging in and just assume she will give you what you need to know. You have to make friends with her first, I mean with Sherry Taylor, then and only then, will she introduce you to Tracy Wells. It's common with personality disorders for them to be protective of their other selves."

"Is that all Miss Moore?"

"Yes Sir."

Strain re-entered the interview room, sat down and switched on the tape. He named everyone who was present in the room, the date, and the time.

He sat there for a moment thinking about what Sandy Moore had said. He knew that she was right, again.

In a calm voice he asked: "Could you confirm for me that your name is Sherry Taylor."

She nodded her answer.

"For the purpose of the tape - I need you to say it out loud."

"Yes, my name is Sherry Taylor."

"Do you know why we have brought you here today, Sherry? May I call you Sherry?"

She nodded again. "Well, although we've never met, I don't feel like we are strangers, DCI Strain, having said that I'm disappointed to find Sergeant Wilding missing from the room, or is he out pretend jogging. You must think I was born yesterday. Yes, you can call me Sherry, and the only reason I am here is because you have arrested me. Apparently, you think I've committed murder, which is totally outrageous. Why do you think I killed Mrs Johnson? I loved her." Her voice was starting to get louder. "She was everything to me, like the mother I never had."

"You did have a mother though, Sherry, didn't you?"

"I've never had a mother, not one that I can remember," she said quietly. "My sister and I were orphaned at a very young age." She sat there twisting her fingers together. "But things turned out ok and I have been very happy."

"And yet I am led to believe that you had a somewhat tragic childhood. Isn't that right, Sherry, would you agree with me on that?"

The duty solicitor leaned in and spoke quietly to Sherry, but as she turned to face him, she snapped at him. "Well, I do want to answer. I have nothing to hide."

She turned back to face Strain. "No, I do not agree with you, I had a very happy childhood, thank you Detective Chief Inspector!"

"So, what you are saying is that you didn't murder your parents when you were ten years old?"

"No, of course not, why would you say that? That's a terrible accusation to make."

She turned to her Solicitor. "Why are you allowing him to make these false allegations about me. Aren't you going to stop him. I didn't kill anyone. I loved my parents."

"So you do remember having parents?" Strain was pushing harder.

"Stop it. You're confusing me. I have a vague memory of my parents, but I didn't kill them."

She sat there in silence for a few moments and then added in a quiet voice, "it wasn't me - it was Tracy!"

"Are you not Tracy? Tracy Wells?" Strain asked maintaining an even tone.

She sat up in her seat and said in a raised voice, "No, I'm not Tracy. I'm Sherry for goodness sake, what's wrong with you?" She glared at him with rage.

"Have you known Tracy for a long time? Are you still friends? Do you keep in touch with her?" He hoped this wasn't too much for her to take in.

"Yes, I've known Tracy all my life. We were childhood friends." She fell silent, eyes glistening from the memory. "Would you like to meet Tracy? You can if you want to. She's probably not far away. I hadn't seen her for such a long time but just recently she has started to visit me again, which is nice. I hadn't realised how much I missed her."

"So, who is Tracy, and where is she now?

"She's my friend, my special friend, and I don't think she wants to meet you. But I'll ask her." Sherry sat there staring at the wall and stayed in this trance like state for quite a few minutes.

Strain exchanged a glance with her solicitor, as he heard a voice he wasn't familiar with.

"I am right here. I'm always here!" Sherry had turned her head back and was looking directly at him, then, within seconds she had jumped to her feet and launched herself across the table at Strain and screamed, "I'm Tracy and I'm the one responsible for the death of that stupid old woman. Do you understand? It's my fault she's dead, not Sherry's. Do not blame her. It was me. Do you hear?" Then she slumped back onto her chair.

Strain remained outwardly calm and sat quietly, observing as her face flushed red and contorted.

"I went to see the pathetic old bitch. I only wanted to chat with her for a while to see why Sherry loved her so much, but it got out of hand. She kept on calling me Sherry and asking me what was wrong with me. She didn't believe that I wasn't Sherry and that my name was Tracy. She said I had gone crazy, and she just kept crying and telling me to leave. She reminded me of my parents. They were weak and pathetic too. And then the stupid whimpering woman had some sort of funny turn. Weak people, I hate them. You have to believe me when I tell you it wasn't Sherry there on that night, it was me, and I didn't kill the stupid woman, she died in hospital." Her tone of voice changed slightly and became almost childlike as she muttered over and over, "I'm so sorry Sherry. I'm so sorry Sherry. You're really happy for the first time in your life and now I've gone and spoilt it for you. And for a moment there she almost sounded sad, but then her temper flared again, and she began shouting, "It was my fault. You need to punish me.

Strain indicated that he needed the presence of officers to restrain her while she wailed.

When everyone had left the interview room, Strain called Rob on his mobile to confirm that he had finished interviewing Christie. He didn't want to run the risk of bumping into her in the corridor.

Rob answered and confirmed that she had gone.

CHAPTER FIFTY-ONE

Rob caught up with strain and they walked to the office together. As they did so, he briefed Strain on his interview with Christie, but clearly it was all out in the open now as Sherry Taylor, or Tracy Wells as she'd been born, had confessed to indirectly causing the death of Mrs Johnson.

"Bit of a shocker," said Rob.

"I know, quite unnerving really. I'm not sure any of us are ever in full control of our own minds. It's complicated stuff. Anyway, let's look on the bright side. At least one of our cases is solved."

Strain seemed to have this ability to sweep over things; dot the I's and cross the T's, case closed. But for Rob, it went deeper than that and he thought he might actually have nightmares over Sherry Taylor's sinister side for quite some time to come.

"Right, see you later. I'm off to brief Chief Superintendent Ridley."

Rob went to get himself a drink. He spotted Sophie standing in the corridor with her back to him. So, very slowly, on tiptoe, he crept up behind her, wrapped his arms around her waist and spun round in a circle with her. She shrieked with laughter and said, "You're in a fun mood."

She couldn't have been further from the truth.

As Rob stopped spinning and put her down, she reached her hand up and touched the top of her head to make sure her glasses were still there. and they both quickly looked to see if anyone was watching them frolicking, but nobody was.

"Actually, 'fun mood' isn't the right description, but we have solved one of our cases, so how do you fancy celebrating with me tonight?"

"I would love to" she said beaming.

"Great. I'll see you after work" he said and kissed her.

He helped himself to a cup of cold water from the dispenser and went back to the office.

Sophie watched him as he walked away. "Now this is more like it," she said under her breath. "Maybe I won't have to dump him after all. Tonight could be the night. He has been a gentleman for far too long."

CHAPTER FIFTY-TWO

When Strain returned to the office, he was surprised to see Rob sitting at his desk. "Why are you still here? I would have thought you'd be long gone by now. Aren't you off out celebrating with your girlfriend tonight?" He put the files down onto his desk and added, "Are you still seeing Sophie?"

"Yes and yes, but I'm just sorting out this report," he replied without looking up.

"Why not leave it until tomorrow?" Strain asked.

"Thanks, but I would rather do the paperwork straight away, while it's fresh in my mind, then it's finished and done with. Besides, I think I might be in therapy tomorrow, and it'll take a bloody good councillor to help me forget what I witnessed this afternoon." He gave Strain a half-hearted smile. "I can't shift the image of Sherry Taylor's transformation out of my mind. For one person to actually become two people right in front of you, it's possibly the most disturbing scene I have ever had the misfortune to witness. He shook his head as if that might somehow clear the image from his mind. "Anyway, as soon as I'm done here, I'm meeting up with Sophie."

Rob let out an irritated sigh. "Actually, Guv, I can't go after I've done this paperwork. I've just thought, I still need to contact, 'The Lantern Bistro bar' in New Road and talk to them regarding our latest victim, Tom Lewis."

Strain sat down at his desk, "Don't worry about that, Rob, I'll go."

Rob raised his eyebrows: "Are you sure you don't mind?"

"Of course not. It's not like I have anywhere else to be. My relationship with Christie is now well and truly in tatters." He tried to make light of it but inside he was gutted at the thought of not seeing her again.

He picked up the file containing the notes on the events leading up to the murder of Tom Lewis and read through them. As he pushed his chair out and got up, he said: "Right, Rob, I'll leave you to your report. I'm going to head over to New Road and see if I can de-mist Tom's final movements."

"Thanks Guv. Call me if you need me. I'll have my mobile on."

Strain nodded and left the office.

CHAPTER FIFTY-THREE

As Strain parked his car, he could see that there were lights on inside the old Victorian building. He pushed on the entrance door, and it opened. Inside there were people milling around, polishing tables, and moving chairs. At the bar area there was a young man stacking glasses who nodded to Strain.

"Can I help you mate?"

"DCI Strain," he said, holding out his ID Card. "Are you the Manager?"

"I am," he replied as he stopped what he was doing and stood upright. "How can I help you?"

"I'm investigating the murder of this young man, "he said, showing him a picture of Tom Lewis. "He was dropped off here by Taxi last night. Do you recognise him at all?"

The manager looked at the image on Strain's phone.

"Hmm, sorry mate, I can't be certain, it's manic in here every night. Do you want to look at the CCTV?"

"Yeah, that would be good, thank you." Strain followed him into an office that was the size of a shoe box, with barely enough room for a desk, chair, filing cabinet and two people. He watched as the manager rolled back the recording to the opening times of the previous day. He gave Strain a quick lesson on how to stop, start, fast forward, rewind and freeze the frame. He pulled the chair out for him and asked him if he would like anything to drink and then he left him to it.

Strain sipped the coffee he had been given as he scrutinised the footage. He was already beginning to regret his decision to stand in for Rob. It was such a tedious task, and it took a lot of concentration to stare at a screen hoping to spot something of interest, something that might catch his eye. Just then something did. He sat up in his chair and pulled it closer to the desk. "Well, I'll be..." he said under his breath, "What have we got here?" He watched it through to the end with renewed interest. He called the manager back in and asked him for a copy. The young man obliged him and Strain left the club wondering what the hell was wrong with these women.

CHAPTER FIFTY-FOUR

Kim Carmichael entered the police station and with an overwhelming feeling of pride she walked over to the reception desk, although her pride did nothing to quell the butterflies that were flying around in her stomach. "Excuse me," she asked the desk sergeant. "Could you tell me where the human resources office is located, please?" Her first interview had been almost twelve months earlier at the police training college in Worcestershire, and as a successful candidate, she had gone on to complete her training and pass with credits. The next stage of the process was for her to apply to a police force of her choice, and naturally she wanted to work in her hometown, so when a formal brown envelope had landed on her door mat, she had been over the moon. She had eagerly ripped it open to find it contained an invitation requesting her attendance at an interview doing just that, so there was a lot riding on this early evening meeting.

"I certainly can," the cheery-faced sergeant said. "It's on the third floor and the lift is just along here." He indicated the direction with his finger. "Towards the far end of this corridor on the left. If you prefer to take the stairs, keep going past the lift and you will see them."

"Thanks very much," Kim replied, walking off with an air of excitement fizzing around her. Ever since she was a child, she had wanted to join the police force, and now here she was, hopefully, about to realise her dream.

"Good luck," he called after her.

Kim turned back and smiled her acknowledgement at him before making her way towards the stairs. Given the choice this would always be hers, thanks to the film, *Towering Inferno,* which had left her non too keen on lifts. As she walked along the corridor and then up the stairs, she began going over in her mind, for about the fortieth time, what she thought she might be asked and what her answer would be. She knew it was just nerves, and that she'd be okay once the interview began. She pushed open the door from the stairwell and stepped into a corridor that had a large sign on the wall that silently announced her arrival at the Human Resources Department. She turned her head to a young woman who was walking towards her and stopped suddenly as she recognised her. She was wearing thick rimmed glasses, but Kim was sure it was her. "Hello," she said, a lot louder than she meant to. "How are you? Or rather, how's your knee, or was it your ankle? I can't quite remember now what your injury was, but I never forget a face."

The woman didn't respond. She just stood there with a puzzled look on her face.

"I'm Kim! Don't you remember me? We jogged together that one time, a few months back, in Hinton Woods, and you tripped over and hurt yourself and those two men helped you and escorted us back to your car. Ringing any bells yet? I'm actually still friends with both of them. We became jogging buddies and we regularly run together, surely you remember?"

The girl standing in front of her looked extremely uncomfortable and Kim could see she had clenched her fists as she shook her head in a dismissive way. But Kim knew she hadn't made a mistake. Even though she was wearing thick glasses, she could easily recognise her.

"Anyway, I'm glad to see you made a full recovery. I'm sorry to be rude but I've got to dash. I have an interview. Maybe, if I get the job, I'll see you again. That is if you work here. Or maybe you would like to join our little jogging group."

Slightly miffed at the lack of response, Kim decided she had more important matters to deal with rather than wasting her time talking to someone who clearly wasn't interested in talking to her, so she turned and walked away.

"Bye," the girl called after her. "Best of luck," she added under her breath.

"Hey Sophie"

Sophie turned around as she heard her name, and saw Rob walking towards her:

"Have you finished for the day? I've just got to finish writing up a report, and then I'm done. Shall I come over to yours then, save you hanging around here waiting for me."

She swiftly pushed her glasses up onto the top of her head and replied, "Yes that's a great idea, I'll see you at mine. She felt her fists relax and she forced a smile, but she knew this chance meeting with Kim was a game changer.

CHAPTER FIFTY-FIVE

It had taken Rob a lot longer than he had anticipated, so he was pleased that Sophie had already gone home rather than hanging around at work waiting for him. He took his phone from his pocket and sent her a text. It pinged back at him with a reply of, 'Yes, I'm waiting patiently, actually, impatiently, for you.' She had ended the sentence with a smiling emoji, with hearts for eyes. It made him feel good to read her display of affection and he grabbed his jacket and left the office feeling happy.

At home he showered, dressed, and set up Google map with Sophie's address on his mobile phone. He'd not been to her house before, but he was familiar with the new estate. The journey there took him about thirty minutes and when he arrived, he parked up on the roadside and walked up the black tarmac drive, casting his eyes over the front of her house. He stood at the door and at the exact same moment that he went to press the doorbell it opened and she was standing there, in front of him, looking very pretty. She immediately leaned in and kissed him.

He kissed her back and when he pulled away, said, "Hi you."

"Hey" she said, smiling up at him.

She took his hand and led him inside her house where she kissed him again. She looked up at him and said, "Anything you fancy doing before we go out to eat?"

He grinned at her and in a low voice whispered, "maybe," closing the front door and pulling her into his arms, they continued to kiss for a while before she gently pulled away and took him upstairs.

Passion spent, they lay quietly, wrapped in each other's arms, until Sophie broke their contented silence. "Are you hungry? Because I am. Shall we get dressed and go out for something to eat?"

Given the choice, Rob would have happily stayed right where they were for the rest of the night, but not wishing to appear selfish he replied, "Absolutely. Where would you like to go?"

She kissed him on the cheek and said, "No idea. You can have a think while I have a quick shower," and she left the room.

Rob lay there with his hands behind his head feeling totally relaxed. So much so, that he thought he might fall asleep. He sat up and looked around the bedroom at his clothes that were scattered all over the floor. He too wanted a shower before he got dressed, so he sat on the end of her bed waiting for her to finish in the bathroom.

He heard the shower stop and began to gather up his things. As he bent down to pick up his shirt, he saw his jeans by the side of an open box in the corner by her dressing table. He picked them up and without meaning to be nosy, he looked inside and pulled out a large handful of chiffon scarves. He heard the bathroom door open and quickly dropped them back inside and took his place on the end of the bed. As Sophie came into the bedroom, he thought he saw her face tense up slightly, like she could sense something was wrong. Trying to act normal, he spotted the towel she was holding, "Is that for me?"

She nodded and chucked the clean towel at him. "Yes. The bathroom is the next door along on the right."

As he left the room, he saw her eyes dart to the open box of scarves. He heard her sigh as she swore quietly under her breath.

She quickly dressed and went downstairs, spotting Robs jacket by the front door, she rummaged through the pockets until she found his mobile phone, switched it off, and put it back in his pocket. She poured a small glass of white wine for each of them, and dropped two small white pills into Robs, swishing it around until they had dissolved, then she waited in the kitchen for him.

When he eventually joined her, she said, "Ready to go and eat?"

"Yes," he lied. "Unless you fancy a takeaway, and the rest of the night back in your bed."

His mind had gone into overdrive after his discovery. He thought if he offered to fetch them some takeout food, he would be able to ring Strain and tell him what he had found.

"As long as I get to spend it with you, I don't mind what we do." She smiled and handed him his drink. She leaned up and kissed him, then clinked her glass to his.

"Cheers" Rob said and drank the contents.

CHAPTER FIFTY-SIX

Hilary Turner, head of human resources, was sitting at her desk. The first hopeful was due to attend her final interview in approximately ten minutes time. The second list of qualifying applicants had been updated and she had just finished printing off the full list of call backs.

She loved it when months of hard work and decision making came to fruition.

As she glanced through the list she frowned and read it again, "well that's weird," she said quietly.

Feeling puzzled she read through the document she was holding once more, but she was still totally mystified at what she may have discovered. She got up and walked straight past Kim, who was sitting waiting patiently, and headed into the lift. A few minutes later she arrived at CID and stood outside Strain's office. She paused in the doorway, and knocked, even though it was open.

When there was no reply she poked her head through the doorway to find he was not at his desk.

"Why are they never around when you need them," she grumbled to herself as she took the lift back to her floor.

She arrived back at her office and once again she walked past Kim. She sat down and thought for a moment, unsure of what to do with this information. She chewed on her lip and suddenly became aware of the young lady sitting in the waiting area. She signalled to her that she would only be a moment then picked up her phone and dialled Strain's number.

It went straight to answer service.

"DCI Strain, it's Hilary here from HR, I need to have a word with you, it's important, so if you could give me a call back when you get this message, I would appreciate it. Thanks."

She replaced the receiver, gathered up the paperwork and put it to one side then she got up, straightened her skirt, and walked over to the young lady who was waiting for her.

"I'm Hilary Turner," she said, offering her hand forward. "I'm sorry to have kept you waiting."

CHAPTER FIFTY-SEVEN

Strain arrived back at the office, grabbed himself a cup of coffee and sat down at Rob's desk. He inserted the USB stick into the computer and once again watched the CCTV footage he had brought back from the Lantern Bar.' He pressed pause and stared at the screen. The picture clearly showed Sophie, Rob's girlfriend, sitting on a bar stool, laughing, chatting, and drinking with their latest murder victim, Tom Lewis. He rubbed the side of his neck, got up and went out into the corridor. He knew Sophie wouldn't still be at work at this time of night, but he had a look around, just in case. He returned to his office and sat back down. He pressed play and watched again as they shared just over an hour together before leaving the bar - together!

Strain took his phone out of his pocket to call Rob but just at that moment, Hilary, from human resources walked in, holding up some paperwork.

"DCI Strain, thank goodness."

"Hilary," he said, thinking she might be here to moan at him. "I'm sorry, something important came up, and I..."

"That's not the reason I'm here. Didn't you get my message."

He didn't let on that he had ignored it, instead he feigned a puzzled look on his face.

"I need to show you something that I discovered earlier. I think it may be important." She moved and stood at the side of him.

"What's up?" he asked, giving her his full attention.

"I printed off a full list of call-backs. I also printed off a list of all the people that we have interviewed during the last twelve months, to use as a comparison, to avoid any errors."

Patience had never been his strong point and he had no idea what she was rambling on about, or what it was leading to.

Hilary turned the list to face him. "Look see here. I went through each candidate and highlighted the individuals that had been earmarked for a second interview, only to discover something very disturbing."

As Strain waited for the big reveal, he cast his eyes over the piece of paper she was holding and snatched it from her. "What the...? Why have you got a piece of paper with three of my murder victim's names written on it?."

"Well, Sir, that's what I am trying to tell you, three out of the five women we had shortlisted are dead!"

As he stared at the piece of paper, his thoughts were interrupted by the appearance of Sandy Moore.

"I'm looking for Rob, is he here?"

"No," Strain said, "you've missed him. He's out on a date with Sophie."

Sandy opened her mouth to reply, but Hilary beat her to it.

"With Sophie Longfellow, our cleaning lady? How lovely. She's such a nice girl. Do you remember when she applied to join the police force? It was a few years ago now, but because she suffers from a severe colour vision deficiency, Monochromacy, I think it was called, she was unfortunately denied a position.

Strain couldn't remember. He thanked Hilary for the list and he leaned back in his chair, leaving the two women chatting together. This is the link, he thought. The one thing the murdered girls had in common was that they wanted to join the police force, and they had made it to round two. As he looked at the computer screen in front of him, he was reminded that Sophie was now a person of interest, and she would have to be brought in for questioning.

He dialled Rob's number, but it went to voicemail. "Come on, Rob," he muttered under his breath, "you know better than to switch your phone off." He left a message telling him to get back to the station and to bring Sophie with him. He got up and updated the incident board with the new information. He wondered why Rob had not turned up this information before now, with all the background checks that he had conducted on the victims, he really should have made this discovery weeks ago. Once again he rang Rob's mobile. "For fucks sake Rob, call me back!"

He was starting to feel agitated as he sat back down and looked over at the incident board. He looked at the faces of the victims, pre-murder. He looked at the locations in which they were killed and at the lack of evidence at every crime scene. He looked at the photos, post-murder, where the victim's eyes were covered with a scarf.

And then it hit him, in bold capitals. "Fucking hell!"

Both Hilary and Sandy looked over at him.

"Sorry ladies," he said. It's her, she's our serial killer. Do we know the registration number of her car?"

"Whose?" Both women said in unison.

"Sophie Longfellow," Strain shouted. "She's our serial killer and she's been right here under our noses the whole time. Rob said only this morning that he had been surprised when he'd bumped into her a few days ago out jogging in Ringwood, and even though he's been dating her, up until then he had no idea that she went jogging. It's her and she's with Rob!"

Strain reached into his pocket for his mobile and called Rob for a third time. Again it went straight to voicemail, Strain bellowed into the phone, as if shouting louder would make him more likely to answer. "Call me back as soon as you get this message, Rob, its important!"

He turned to Sandy. "Get a squad car and go with them round to Rob's house, they'll know where he lives and if there's no answer, don't hold back - break the door down!" Sandy nodded and turned on her heel.

"Hilary, I need you to get her address and car registration for me and her mobile phone number."

"Yes Sir," she said and strode off down the corridor.

She was back within minutes and handed Strain the information he'd asked for.

Strain knew Rob would never purposely ignore his phone, or have it switched off, so he must be in trouble.

He rang down to the desk sergeant and told him he needed a couple of squad cars to assist him immediately.

They were waiting out the front by the time Strain got outside.

He ran to his car and took off at speed, followed closely by the uniformed officers.

He hoped he would find the both of them at Sophie's house, he didn't think Rob would take a girl back to his place, after only a handful of dates. But nevertheless, his address had to be checked out, and although, for whatever reason, Sandy Moore constantly annoyed him, he knew she could cope with the task.

They arrived at the property Hilary had given him the address of and parked up on the kerb.

There was an Audi parked on it and the reg matched what he had written down.

"Check the car," Strain called out to one of the officers as he got out of his vehicle.

He rushed up the drive and knocked aggressively on the front door.

CHAPTER FIFTY-EIGHT

As Strain knocked repeatedly, a neighbour opened her window and shouted, "Blimey, where's the fire, what's going on?" Without waiting for a reply she added, "If you're looking for the woman who lives there, she's not in!"

"Do you know where she might be?" Strain asked.

"No, I don't know where they went but I saw her helping some guy into a car about forty-five minutes ago. To be honest he looked a bit drunk, which I guess is why she was driving. Why, what's she done?"

Ignoring her question, Strain said, "Just close your windows and lock your doors for now. If you have children, it would be best to keep them indoors with you."

The neighbour hastily shut her window and disappeared.

"Sophie Longfellow, can you hear me, it's DCI Strain. Can you open the door, I need to have a word with you?"

When no reply came back he shouted to one of the uniformed police officers: "Break it down!"

An officer stepped forward and using his door ram he aimed close to the door handle.

As the front door crashed open, Strain pushed past the officer and was the first one to enter the house. His eyes flashed around the downstairs rooms, quickly taking in his surroundings. There was a computer on the table with an autumnal screen saver picture of woodland. A leather sofa, a coffee table and a television were the only other pieces of furniture. Two of the officers went upstairs and two went outside into the back garden.

Strain walked into the kitchen. It was neat and tidy, except for two wine glasses on the work surface next to the sink. He visually examined them. One had lipstick on and a small amount of wine left in it, and the other one had, what looked like, a residue of powder in the bottom. "Christ, Rob what has she done to you?" he said under his breath.

Just then, one of the officers came into the kitchen and said, "Guv, you need to see this, upstairs."

Strain followed him up the stairs and into a small bedroom which was kitted out with a complete home gym.

"In here, Guv," a voice called out from the other bedroom. Strain joined him and the officer pointed to an open box that he had found in the corner of the room next to a dressing table. Using a gloved hand he revealed the contents to be chiffon scarves!

"She's definitely our murderer!" Strain said.

"Down here, Guv," an officer called up from the open front door.

As he left the room he said, "Secure these rooms, call forensics, and get them here to do a sweep." He went back downstairs and outside to Sophie's car.

The officer who had found the car unlocked, opened the boot to reveal a neat row of tool kits, several rolls of duct tape, black bags, and a pair of leather gloves. "I don't need to tell you to secure this vehicle." Strain said.

The officer that had checked the garden appeared behind him. "Shed, Sir."

Strain followed him back through the house and out into the garden. As he stepped inside the shed he was amazed by what he saw.

The walls were covered with a diary of events. Sophie Longfellow had certainly done her research.

There were pictures of the murdered victims, along with running times and dates. Notes had been left beside them stating: 'unnecessary', 'unsuccessful', 'rescheduled', or 'successful'.

There was a newspaper cutting of Holly Jones and written underneath, gone but not forgotten - never to be found.

As his eyes took in this information, he thought about Rob and how much danger he was in.

"Where now," Strain said to anyone who might be listening. He walked back to the house and into the lounge. He took a clean protective glove from his pocket and moved to the computer. He touched the mouse and the picture on the screen disappeared, revealing a Google map with a red pointer on it. He clicked on it and enlarged it.

"Mary-way Woodland Park," he shouted. "Come on, let's go! Someone needs to stay here and keep this house, the back garden, and her car secure with its evidence until forensics arrive and be watchful in case she returns."

"I'll do it, Guv," a voice replied.

"And radio for back-up to Mary-way Woods. As many officers as possible."

CHAPTER FIFTY-NINE

It seemed to take forever to get to Mary-way Woods but finally Strain followed the sign off the dual carriageway and down to a round-about. He took the first left off the main road and through the entrance that led to the ranch style carpark. He could see Rob's car parked in the far corner. As he got out, the officers and the back-up he had requested all arrived within minutes of each other. Mary-way woods were small in comparison to other local woodland, so Strain made the decision to send his officers and the four back-up cars away to cover the other entrances and exits and carry out their search from different angles.

"Get a move on and keep in touch with me," he told them.

The night was drawing in and they were rapidly losing the light, which would undoubtedly hinder their search. As he entered the woodland he called Rob's mobile, just in case, but it was switched off.

"Come on Rob, where are you?" He cursed under his breath. This was not going to be an easy search. He was beginning to regret his decision to send his back up away, he should have kept one guy with him.

As he walked along the pathway his eyes scanned to the left, to the right and straight ahead. He resisted the urge to call out to Rob, for fear of alerting Sophie.

Not knowing which way to go he stopped and thought for a moment, he rummaged through his pocket for the piece of paper that Hilary had given him with Sophie's details on, and although he could barely see to read it, he managed to punch her number into his phone.

He stopped to listen and heard it ringing somewhere to his left. It stopped almost immediately, so he rang it again. He listened hard, just two rings, but definitely to his left.

He came off the pathway, rang it again and walked quickly towards the sound before it stopped. It was leading him into the thicket, and he carefully picked his way through the under growth. It was hard walking through the overgrown clumps of bracken.

He stopped and caught his breath as a short distance ahead he could see something, "what on earth is that over there," he said under his breath.

As he got closer, he thought he could see two shoes sticking up through some wild heather, panicking slightly he called out: "Oh my god, Rob."

He tried to run and as he trod down the brambles they clung onto his trousers and ripped through the material. His hands and legs were buzzing from the scratches, and it seemed to be taking an eternity to reach Rob, if indeed it was Rob. His heart was beating erratically as he called out to him. "Rob, is that you, can you hear me?" There were no replies but finally Strain came to a stop and as he stood over the body lying in front of him, he could see there was a chiffon scarf covering his face.

"Jesus Christ, Rob!" Strain yelled as he pulled the scarf off his face. Even though it was dark he could see a pool of blood was forming underneath Rob's head. He felt for a pulse and dialled 999:

"This is DCI Strain. I need an ambulance immediately; the victim has a faint pulse and a suspected head injury, we are at Mary-way Woodland Park, East entrance. Maybe you can follow the tracker on my phone to find us and I'm sure I don't need to tell you to be quick about it - but it's for one of our own." Strain took off his jacket and placed it carefully over Rob to keep him warm. He knelt down by his side and checked his pulse again. A sudden pain took him by surprise. It felt as though his head had been burst open.

CHAPTER SIXTY

Strain blinked his eyes repeatedly as he began to regain consciousness. He had a searing pain in his head, and his hands were tied behind his back. It was dark, but as his eyes began to focus he found himself looking directly at Sophie. Gone was the sweet girl that worked in the same building as he did and, in her place, staring back at him was a cold-faced girl with a snarling mouth.

"Sophie," Strain said, "what are you doing?"

"Shut up, you useless dickhead. I can't believe that I'm the one who got turned down and denied a place in the force because my vision isn't 100%, but you couldn't even see what was going on right under your nose, you useless arrogant twat!"

"Is that what this is all about, Sophie? You killed all those innocent people just because they were more successful than you would ever be? What were you thinking; you must have known that we would catch up with you eventually?"

He could hear sirens in the distance, but he knew they would be a while yet, because he could see his phone lying on the ground smashed to pieces, which meant the tracker would have been disabled.

"But I already have. I have been getting away with it for a long time and I would have continued to get away with it for a lot longer if it hadn't been for Miss clever clogs - Kim Carmichael - the one that got away!"

Strain recalled reading that name on the wall in her shed.

"I have watched you scratching your head and pawing over the crime scenes, with nothing to go on except dead bodies. Those are just the ones you know about and that's only because I wanted you to know. I wanted you to see them. Yes, that's right. Because you would never have been clever enough to find them yourself."

Trying to buy some time Strain asked, "Who is Kim Carmichael, Sophie, what's she got to do with you?"

"I bumped into her at the station today, she was coming in for her interview, and she recognised me from the night I had planned to murder her but due to unforeseen circumstances, she got to live on. I always knew that one day her lucky escape would come back and bite me on the arse."

"What happened to Holly Jones? Where is she? Is she still alive?"

"Oh, the stupid opinionated news-reader bitch. She thought she knew the answers to everything, didn't she? Fucking know-all. You'll never find her!" She leered at him.

"But is she still alive, Sophie?"

"Shut up, I'm not telling you anything. You're not in charge here, I am! And she deserved everything that happened to her."

"Okay, but what about Rob, Sophie? I thought you liked him. Surely you wouldn't want to hurt him. He looks like he's in a bad way and he might die if he doesn't get urgent medical help."

"Stop being so patronising. You're talking to me like I'm an idiot. I'm not bothered about him. He's nothing to me. It's not personal," she laughed, "I just used him to get to you. I tried to extract snippets of information from him regarding your murder investigation, but he was so freaking loyal to you, and he never let anything slip. It was another waste of my time." She laughed through her words as she looked down at Rob: "I think the correct term for it is collateral damage!"

Through the moonlight, Strain could see that her eyes were wild, revealing the true psycho that had been cleverly hiding.

"You are the one solely responsible for the deaths of your future recruits because you are the one that signed off on my application as an unsuitable candidate, apparently, due to my sight defect. All these deaths are your fault - how does that make you feel, DCI Strain?"

He vaguely remembered rejecting an applicant due to an eye defect, but his decision hadn't been based solely on her medical condition. Her qualifications weren't up to scratch. There had been applicants a lot more deserving than she had been. She was right about one thing though, he was a dickhead, why hadn't he remembered her.

"Explain to me, please, just how being colour blind makes me any less able to do the job than you?" She paused for a moment. "What's the matter, DCI Strain, it's not like you to have nothing to say."

She stood there staring at him for a few seconds before saying, "Actually, now I come to think of it, I did feel a small amount of guilt over the barman, Tom. He was nice, and a great lay, but I did that to make you suspect that your lawyer girlfriend might just be in the mix. And it worked, didn't it? For a while there, I had you all messed up in your head. Anyway, if you'll excuse me, as much as I would love to stay and chat, Guv, I have to get going before your troops arrive."

As she turned to leave, her legs suddenly buckled beneath her, sending her crashing down into the under-growth. A scream escaped from her mouth as she landed heavily in the bracken. Thorns stabbed at her face and got caught in her hair. She struggled to get to her feet but before she could move someone had pulled her arms behind her back and handcuffed them firmly together.

"What the fuck?" She growled.

Sandy Moore rolled Sophie over to face her. "I'd stick to cleaning if I were you, love. There's always more than one reason why some people don't make the team!"

Sophie tried to kick her legs up into the air, but Sandy was too quick, and she managed to restrain her.

"You fucking bitch! I'm going to put you with Holly Jones when I get out of these cuffs!"

Happy that Sophie Longfellow was secure. Sandy walked over to Strain.

"Hey there, Guv, how's it going?"

"I've been better. Do you think you could untie me, Miss Moore?"

"Oh please, call me Sandy!" she said sarcastically, obliging him with his request and helping him to his feet.

Strain lost his balance and struggled to stand unattended. Sandy took hold of his arm and helped to support him. She left him leaning on a tree and checked on Rob.

She was just about to take her coat off and place it over him when a torch light appeared up ahead. It was the paramedics, accompanied by several police officers.

Two of the officers lifted Sophie to her feet and held her by each arm as they walked her slowly out of the wood.

The paramedics attended to Rob and stretchered him off to the ambulance. They offered to come back for Strain, but he declined their assistance and with a helpful arm from Sandy, managed to walk back along the path to the car park where the ambulance was waiting. They insisted on taking him to the hospital to check his head wound. He agreed under protest, but before he got into the waiting vehicle he stood and watched his team as they silently took the serial killer into custody. They were clearly shocked, that this woman, who had worked in their station, could be responsible for so many murders.

Sandy left Strain with the paramedics and began to walk away.

"Damn good job, Miss Moore" he called after her.

"Thank you, Sir.

CHAPTER SIXTY-ONE

It was a cool but sunny Monday morning when Rob arrived at work. He had been on sick leave for six weeks and was looking forward to returning to normal life. As he walked through the familiar office door and over to his desk, he was greeted by his colleagues who gave him a round of applause. He felt a bit embarrassed by their actions and he blushed slightly, but it felt good to be back and part of a team once again. He'd had a lot of time to think, during his recovery, about his future and where he wanted to be and he had decided that major crimes wasn't for him, so he had put in a request for a transfer back to his previous unit. Although, Strain had opposed it, it had been accepted by the Chief Super, and here he was back in his old job, in the fraud squad. He had given his decision a lot of consideration and realised that he wasn't cut out for CID. For starters, dating a murderer hadn't been the smartest move and he wasn't sure he would ever live that one down.

He placed his jacket on the back of his chair and sat down at his desk and for the first time in what seemed like a long time, he felt like he belonged.

Word had got out that Rob had been worrying about Sherry Taylor's cat and what might happen to him, and he had offered to give him a home. Strain had told him he was, "A big soft idiot."

"Yes, I am" Rob had replied "and very happy to be." So they had handed the cat over to him as a leaving present.

Back at CID, on Rob's recommendation, at exactly eight twenty-five a.m. Steve Miller fetched a coffee for his boss. As he put it down on his desk, he heard a loud voice shouting from the corridor. He turned to look at the door as it opened:

"Steve, I presume," said Strain "nice to meet you: What have you got for me?"

"Coffee, milk, one sugar," Steve replied.

Strain picked up the steaming hot mug: "Thanks Steve, but I meant crimes! What crimes have you got for me?"

"Oh, sorry, Sir."

"I prefer to be called Guv," Strain said.

"Okay, sorry, Sir. Guv."

"Glad we've got that sorted. So other than coffee. What have you got for me?"

EPILOGUE

Christie Harding closed her front door behind her, took off her coat and hung it on a hook in the hallway, she put her bag and car keys down on the small table at the bottom of the stairs and went into the kitchen. It was nice to feel the warmth from her Rayburn and smell the casserole that was slowly cooking in the oven. She pulled out a chair and sat down at the table and put her head in her hands. Taking holiday leave had seemed like the right thing to do, she thought it would enable her to have some alone time and help her to come to terms with everything that had happened. Her life was in tatters. She had no idea how she would be able to carry on knowing that her beautiful sister had lost her right to freedom. She blamed herself completely for what had happened, it was no one else's fault, she was the one solely responsible - she had tried, and she had failed - and she had let Sherry down. Maybe if she had been more attentive then things would have turned out differently. She had cross examined herself over and over again in an attempt to pinpoint what she could have done differently and where it had all gone wrong.

She scraped her hands through her hair and pulled it into a tight ponytail and secured it into place with the band that was on her wrist. As she got up to fill the kettle, she turned to her guest who was sitting in the leather recliner watching the flames flickering from the wood burner.

"Fancy a nice hot drink?" She asked.

"Yes please, that would be lovely, can I have a coffee?"

Christie took two cups from the cupboard and popped a tea bag into one and a teaspoon of coffee into the other: She turned to face her guest and smiled. "It's been so long Tracy; I've forgotten if you take sugar?"

"No, not for me thanks. I'm sweet enough."

Thank you for reading my debut novel, 'In Clear Sight.'
Book two, coming soon, 'Sweet Revenge.'

Best wishes,
Judith Tipping x